Dragons of the Soul

To Graeme,
Hope you like it!

[signature]

BLUE Imp books

For my husband Joel,
and my sons Kyle and Nathan Aaron.
I love you very, very much.

1

A gust rattled the window in Katie Martin's room, and icy snow tapped on the glass like ghostly fingernails. A January snowstorm raged and threatened the entire city.

Katie looked away from the sheet music in front of her and listened to the howling in the darkness outside. She wondered how much snow would be on the ground in the morning. The sixteen-year-old nervously wiped her sweaty palms on her blue jeans. She hoped it would not be too icy at dawn, and already dreaded the nerve-wracking drive to school in the morning.

For now, she needed to practice the clarinet. Katie stared at the odd instrument, as it lay in her lap. Why had she insisted upon a clarinet? She had difficulty keeping the wooden reed moist, but that wasn't the half of it. Her attempts to create sounds resembling musical notes usually resulted in hair-raising squawks. Katie shook her head and sighed.

From the kitchen below, Katie heard the clatter of pots and pans and knew that her mother was starting dinner. She heard her mother's wavy, cheerful hum float up faintly from the lower level of the house.

At least Mom had musical talent. Why hadn't Katie inherited any? *Why did I choose such an impossible instrument? Because you're stubborn Katie, that's why. Now concentrate.* Katie focused on the page and took a deep breath. She sat up straight, and flipped her blonde hair over her shoulders so that it fell to the middle of her back. She determinedly pushed her knitted, blue sweater sleeves up over her elbows, gripped the clarinet in her lap and raised the instrument to her lips. She prepared to produce the first note, and tapped a beat on the light-blue carpet with her sneaker-clad foot.

The phone rang and interrupted Katie's concentration and rhythm. Was it one of her friends? Katie held the clarinet away from her mouth and listened. She heard no shout for her to pick up the phone; the call must be for Mom. Katie raised the clarinet again to her lips, but jerked it away as she heard her mother exclaim, "WHAT?"

Her voice sounded so shocked and loud – so frantic! Katie froze, afraid to breathe. A cold, hard lump formed in the pit of her stomach and a horrid shiver ran up her spine. What happened? Who called?

Katie heard muted sobs. She immediately placed her clarinet on the desk in front of her and rushed from her room to the hallway. She saw Alex, her thirteen-year-old brother, emerge from his room looking worried and tense. He must have heard Mom too. Katie turned and led the way down the short hall to the carpeted stairs. The steps sounded ominous and hollow as she rapidly descended.

At the base of the stairs Katie turned to the left, with her brother following behind, and quickly walked through the den and into the kitchen. Katie gasped when she saw her mother, Audry, seated at the kitchen table. Audry's face looked ghastly pale, as if all color and life had been drained from it.

"Mom! What's wrong?" Katie said as she slid into the chair to Audry's left and reached out for her mother's shaking left hand.

Audry swallowed and looked away from the oak table, slowly, reluctantly up to her daughter's eyes. Katie's breathing quickened with anticipation and worry. Tears rimmed Mom's eyes. Audry released the phone handset, and slowly raised her right hand to cover her thin, trembling lips. Then she clenched her blue eyes shut, and glistening tears leaked out. As the drops streaked down her mother's cheeks, Katie fought her own quivering chin. Audry gripped Katie's right hand so tightly with her left that Katie's knuckles seemed to grind together, and she wanted to withdraw her hand but couldn't. Katie winced and leaned away from her mother, and as she did Alex clamped his hand onto her left shoulder, digging his fingers in.

What happened? Had Aunt Rita, who fought against cancer with every breath, finally lost her battle? Or had death visited Grandma Martin, who just celebrated her eighty-eighth birthday?

"Ty," Audry whispered through the fingers still covering her lips. Katie watched Mom's pretty face scrunch into horrid wrinkles as she began to sob deeply.

It suddenly occurred to Katie that she had not yet heard her eighteen-year-old brother Ty tromp through the front door. Katie glanced warily at the clock on the stove. He should have been home long ago. Had he been in an accident? Had he been badly hurt and now lay in a hospital bed surrounded by beeping machines and bright lights?

"Mom," Katie said as she gripped her mother's left hand with both of hers. Audry's blonde curls quivered as she sobbed. Fear and dread rose within Katie's chest; her heart thumped and her breathing became labored.

"Oh, Katie," Audry sighed as she removed her right hand from her mouth and held both of Katie's hands. Katie searched her mother's eyes, hesitating. She wanted, and yet didn't want, to hear what had happened to her older brother. "Ty was in an accident." Audry struggled, her chin quivering. She swallowed and then continued, her voice barely a whisper, "He's…gone." Audry crumpled over the table and wailed.

"No," Katie breathed; she began to sob. Gone? Did she mean dead? It couldn't be true! She wouldn't believe it — yet why would her mother be so devastated if it wasn't true?

Katie felt Alex's fingers dig farther into her shoulder and heard him crying behind her. She turned to look at him and saw tears trailing down from his brown eyes and over his freckled cheeks.

Audry eased out of her chair and gathered Katie and Alex into her trembling arms. Katie closed her eyes, rested her cheek against her mother's quaking shoulder, and draped her arm across Alex's shoulders as he coughed with sobs.

This can't be! It just can't be real! Katie thought, her mind desperately struggling. Ty was only eighteen! He was a good driver. But the low howling of the wind in the dark world outside mocked her, laughing wickedly.

Katie sniffed; she couldn't breathe through her clogged nose. She ducked away from Audry and Alex and stumbled, dazed, into the den. She snatched a box of tissues from the oak end table. She snagged one and wiped her nose and eyes and brought the box into the kitchen for the others.

Audry swallowed and gathered herself together, straightening her back and squaring her shoulders. "I have to go meet your father," she stated strangely, flatly, without any emotion. Audry absently grabbed her purse from the counter and walked to the closet by the garage door. Katie watched through blurry eyes as Mom clicked the closet door open and pulled her coat from a hanger. She was going to drive in this dangerous weather? How safe would she be in her state of mind? *God give her strength and help her to drive safely,* Katie prayed earnestly.

Katie closed her eyes when her mom stepped near and gently kissed her cheek. Then Katie blinked and saw her mother kiss Alex's forehead. Without another word, Audry opened the door to the garage and slipped through, letting the door thud shut behind her.

Katie stood stunned. Mom had not even suggested that they go with her. She had simply left. Where was she going? Katie wanted to go with her, and yet didn't. The garage door rumbled open and she heard the muted roar of the car's engine. Its sound faded as her mother backed the vehicle onto the street. Seconds later, Katie felt the tremble of the garage door as it rolled shut. Was she going to the hospital? The morgue? Katie didn't know how these things worked, and she didn't want to know.

A frying pan on the stove sizzled and smoked. The ground beef Mom had been cooking began to burn. Katie stepped over to the stove and switched off the heat as she moved the pan to a cold burner. The stove had gone merrily about its business of cooking their dinner. It felt odd.

The whole thing felt odd. It had to be a mistake! Mom and Dad would soon find out that it was somebody else, and Ty had just been delayed because of the bad weather. In fact, he would be coming in through the front door any moment now followed by the cold breath of winter. Katie would hear him stomping snow from his boots and brushing flakes from his coat, and she would rush to him before he could remove his jacket and would grasp him about his waist, and plant her head against his damp chest. He would think it odd that she would embrace him in this manner, but then he would encircle his arms around her and hug her.

The phone rang, bursting Katie's vision of happiness. She walked to the table, picked up the phone and took it to the counter. She didn't want to talk to anybody. She placed the phone in its cradle and looked at the caller ID. It showed "unavailable" and Katie thought it must just be a salesperson.

Katie turned from the counter and realized that Alex no longer stood in the kitchen. Had he gone upstairs? Katie walked through the kitchen and across the corner of the den on her way up to his room, but then she paused when she saw him lying face down on the couch. He gripped a silky gold pillow about his face, weeping into it.

"Alex," Katie spoke. Should she say that everything would be all right? No, she couldn't. She only knelt down next to him and placed her hand on his heaving back.

Alex stopped sobbing for a moment, raised his head from the pillow, and looked at Katie. "What are we going to do?" he asked. Katie didn't know and couldn't answer. She simply shook her head. Alex said, "I'm going up to my room." He sat up, pushed himself off the couch and trudged up the stairs.

Katie stayed in the quiet den for a few minutes, but then walked slowly up the stairs to her bedroom. She softly closed the door behind her and leaned against it. This room had always been her sanctuary, her refuge away from her family, but now it seemed cold and empty.

It all felt so unreal. That morning Ty had been his usual cheerful self. Now he was gone? God, how could this have happened? Why couldn't only bad people have car accidents? Why did good people crash – young people who had their whole lives ahead of them? Katie's mind tumbled with questions she knew she would have to keep to herself because no one could answer them. And because no one could provide answers, the nagging questions continued to roam about in her head unfettered.

Hours later, when she heard the garage door rise, Katie emerged cautiously from her room, her eyes and face puffy from another bout of tears. Katie crept through the hallway and stepped down the stairs. She wanted to hear Mom and Dad say that Ty was okay and that he'd be coming home soon, but her empty stomach pitched when she saw their drawn, pale faces. It was true. Ty was gone.

More hugging. More tears. Alex came downstairs too, and the new family of four held each other and mourned.

Katie's dad, Sam, broke away and cleared his throat, preparing to speak. Would he tell them what happened? Katie feared he would.

"Ty's car," he began, and Katie imagined her brother's old, dark-blue sedan. He was so proud of that car and washed it and shined it every weekend. "It skidded on the ice and crashed head-on into a pole." No airbag — it was too old for an airbag — and in Katie's mind, she saw the pristine car crumpled into wrinkled metal and saw Ty…No! She slammed her eyes shut as if she could keep the image of her fatally injured brother from forming in her mind.

After a few minutes, Mom and Dad told Alex and Katie to get cleaned up and go to bed. They would not go to school tomorrow. They would need time to get through this. Katie reluctantly left her parents and stumbled up the stairs.

In the bathroom, she mechanically washed her face and brushed her teeth. Back in her own room, she undressed, pulled on her flannel pajamas, and rolled into bed.

She couldn't sleep. She lay in bed, thinking. How unfair! In an instant her brother's life had been taken! His life now only existed in her heart and soul as bike rides in the summer heat, speeding up and down dirt trails with the wind tugging their hair. She thought of Christmases with colorful wrapping paper and bows, and painfully realized that in the future the holiday — all holidays — would be without Ty.

She began to wonder if his spirit floated near. Could she feel his presence like a tingle on the back of her neck? Did he watch her? What did he feel? Did he feel as sad as she did that they would never see each other again?

How she wished desperately for one more day, so that she could say something she had never told him. The words had just never come to mind but now they did. She concentrated hard and felt a tingle at the top of her spine. Was he there? Did his spirit hover in the room?

"I love you," Katie whispered, and then she let the tears flow once again. She crumbled back under her covers and pulled her blanket up beneath her chin.

Sleep evaded her. She tossed back and forth, restless. Ty was gone. This thought caused her heart to quicken and made her entire body feel extremely heavy. How much sadness and anguish could one feel? There seemed to be no end to it. She let the heaviness of her body press into the bed. She couldn't sleep. She yawned, but then lay in her bed, her weariness defying her and keeping her awake. Hours passed. She felt as though she should be doing something. But what? What could she do? The one thing she wanted to do – to bring her brother back – was impossible.

Katie shifted to her right side and nuzzled her head into her pillow. Her bedroom door opened slowly and a silhouette stood in her doorway framed by the light from the hallway. The shape looked familiar and she sat up in a start. It was Ty!

Katie raised her arms up wide and motioned for him to come near. With relief flowing through her, she shed tears of happiness.

"Oh, thank God," she whispered, grateful that her brother lived. Ty stepped up to her and wrapped his strong arms around her, hugging her firmly. Katie trembled with joy. "They said you were dead. I couldn't believe it. I wouldn't believe it." She pressed her wet face into his shoulder and nuzzled his arm. She woke. Katie sat up. Where had he gone? Katie wiped tears from her face and pushed up from her damp pillow. *I must have fallen asleep and he went to his room.* Katie quietly opened her bedroom door and slipped into the hallway. She stepped silently down the carpet and wondered why he had disappeared.

Ty's door stood open. Katie's heart beat in her ears as she approached and she entered the dark room, glancing around immediately. Where was he? Katie scanned the room and whispered, "Ty?" She switched on the light. His bed lay empty. His backpack was gone. He wasn't home and Katie suddenly realized that he wouldn't be. She had been fooled. Her own mind had tricked her. Katie crumpled to the floor with profound sadness. She had so desperately wanted to see him again that her subconscious had allowed it to happen, but it wasn't true. She grasped one of his favorite shirts from the end of his bed and held it close, but then wondered why she gripped the cloth so tightly. Was she trying to reach him, wherever he was, through one of the last things he had touched while alive? Katie didn't want to think these things. She felt confused, beaten and foolish. She laid the shirt on the end of his bed and stumbled back down the hallway to her own room. She slowly slid under her covers and tried to sleep.

2

The following morning Katie awoke, blinked and stretched. Had she fallen asleep? She didn't feel rested. She felt stiff, sore and swollen. She lay on her back and watched the brilliant pink and orange glow of the sunrise drift through her curtains. In minutes, the colors faded into a serene yellow. The sun rose, as if no one had died, and dared to shine brightly after such a terrible storm.

Katie got up, tossed on her robe and opened her bedroom door. She smelled the mellow scent of coffee and walked out into the hallway and down the stairs to the kitchen.

Audry put on a brave face and smiled weakly at Katie. Audry stood up from the table, held out her arms and Katie walked up to her, taking the full hug. Sam stood up as well and Katie reached over for him. Her big strong father – he usually towered over them – now seemed shrunken and small. They broke apart and there were no sobs this time. Katie felt relieved; maybe there were no tears left?

Katie noticed papers strewn across the kitchen table. She didn't know what they were and didn't want to know.

"Do you want some juice?" Audry asked. It struck Katie as strange and yet so like her mother. Strange because she said something normal on such an abnormal morning, and so like her because she always looked after her family. Katie didn't want anything to drink. She shook her head and settled into a chair.

Many times she had sat at this table, but not just for meals. They did their homework at this table sometimes, and sometimes just discussed things. They had talked about many problems here. How she wanted to do that now, wanted to talk about how she felt because of the loss of her brother, but she did not want to cause her parents more pain. She knew they would pile her grief on top of their own.

Wistfully Katie thought about how her mom usually settled their worries or resolved their problems. She would call their troubles "dragons." As Katie, Alex or Ty would whine about an upcoming test, or the first day of middle school, or high school, Mom would sweep her sword of encouragement and reassurance gracefully from side to side, and strike down all the fearsome dragons. Then when the discussion neared an end she would always say, "Do you have any more dragons for me to slay?"

Katie desperately wanted to hear her say that now. The biggest, most monstrous dragon stood before her, reared its spiny head and breathed fearsome, fiery breath.

Katie also wanted the normal morning chaos. Instead, they sat at the table in sluggish silence. Audry didn't rush about, sipping her coffee, and her high heels did not click across the kitchen floor. Katie thought she always looked so professional in her nice dresses. Instead, Audry sat sipping her coffee, wearing a robe and slippers and staring with puffy red eyes at the pile of papers.

Sam would normally wear a suit and tie and would cradle his cell phone against his clean-shaven cheek. This morning he wore plaid pajamas, gripped his coffee mug and stared out into space, seeming to be alone with his devastation. Katie suddenly noticed more gray in her father's brown hair. Had it looked that gray yesterday?

Katie excused herself after a few minutes. She thought her parents wanted to talk privately so she left the table and decided she should get a shower. Katie walked up the stairs and back into her room. She slid open drawers and tucked clothing into her arms to carry to the bathroom she shared with her brothers – brother. She walked toward Alex's closed door and paused, pressing her ear against the wood, wondering if Alex was awake yet and wanting to know how he was. She heard nothing, figured he must still be in bed, so she continued down the hall.

She walked quickly past Ty's open bedroom door. She didn't want to look inside, did not want to remember her stupid dream.

In the bathroom, Katie cringed when she saw her face in the mirror. Her blue eyes were red-rimmed and swollen with dark bags underneath. Her normally thin, small nose was red and puffy. She winced and looked down. The first thing she saw was Ty's toothbrush. It was just a toothbrush, but it was obvious and painful. He would never use it again. She reached for it but stopped. What was she doing? Was she going to throw it away? It felt like she'd be tossing Ty into the trash. She quickly withdrew her hand and took a step back, breathing shallowly. She let it be, undressed and got into the shower.

When she was clean and had pulled on blue jeans and her favorite purple sweater, she combed her long, stringy blonde hair out and decided she didn't feel like putting on make-up. She left the bathroom and noticed that Alex's door was open. Alex stood in the middle of his room; he looked confused and lost. He raised his right hand to his head and ran his fingers through his messy brown hair.

"Are you okay?" Katie asked warily.

Alex frowned at Katie and whispered, "He's really gone isn't he?" Then his chin fluttered.

Katie didn't speak. She simply walked up to her little brother, drew him close and hugged him. He felt even thinner than normal. He stood shorter than Katie, but only by a couple of inches. She rested her chin gently on his shoulder as she held him. After a few moments, they released each other and Alex mumbled that he needed to use the bathroom.

Katie left Alex and as she walked down the hall she heard her father's voice from below. He spoke into the phone with low, strained tones, explaining to someone at work why he would not be there today.

"…my son's passing," Katie heard him say, and she felt that he said the words carefully and slowly, as if testing their validity. Was Ty really dead? Did saying so make it more real? She heard Sam say, "Yes, I will," and then his voice broke apart. She heard him say good-bye, then dissolve into deep, hoarse sobs and heard her mother attempting to comfort him.

Her father's crying was the worst. It seemed that men saved all their tears for years and when something awful happened and they could no longer hold it back, all of the pain and sorrow they felt poured out, like a flood from a shattered dam. Katie could count on one hand the times she had seen her father cry, but he had never wept like this.

Katie escaped into her room and closed the door, feeling sobs growing in her own chest once more. She didn't want to cry again.

Katie stayed in her room all morning. She didn't feel like doing anything and only lay on her bed, staring at her ceiling. This was so unfair, but would she rather this had happened to someone else? No. She would not wish this sorrow on anyone. Did God really need him more than they did? He was an angel, so maybe heaven was the place he should be. But Katie's faith was shaken. She wondered why God would allow something like this to happen, and then thought maybe it wasn't God's fault. If everything on earth *were* under God's control, would earth be heaven?

Around noon, Audry gently knocked on Katie's door and asked her if she wanted a sandwich, but even her favorite – bologna and mayo – could not coax her from her room.

Katie remained secluded, privately missing her brother. She knew she would never see Ty's smile again and never experience his gentle, emotional nudging, which often helped put her on the right track. When something would happen to Katie at school, she would talk to Ty; he always seemed to know the right thing to say. He could make you feel better, make you believe you could do anything, just by being yourself. His guidance meant so much to Katie, but now he was gone and that pain was unbearable.

She would never see him again, but Katie convinced herself that the part of him that made him Ty lived on and existed in a different world. She didn't truly understand this, but she felt she must believe it or lose her sanity.

The phone rang in the afternoon. Mom called up the stairs, saying it was Jessie and that she thought Katie should talk with her. Katie wasn't prepared for it but knew she never would be. Who better than her best friend would know how difficult this was?

Katie picked up the extension phone in her room and her throat closed up so tight that she could only croak, "Jessie?"

"Katie, I'm really sorry. I heard about Ty. I'm really sorry." Then Jessie started to cry and Katie found herself sobbing again. Katie envisioned poor Jessie's beautiful, wavy hair trembling with her whimpers.

Jessie had grown up with Katie and her brothers, so losing Ty would – to Jessie – be like losing a brother. But Katie had always suspected something more. She suspected that Jessie had a crush on Ty, although Jessie never admitted it. Jessie would stare at Ty with awe and giggle, and Katie had felt slightly embarrassed for her. Ty thought of Jessie only as his little sister's best friend, no matter how desperately Jessie tried to flirt.

Jessie whispered that she would come to the funeral. Katie nodded and tried to speak a confirming, "uh huh," but it came out high, squeaky and awkward. Katie took a deep breath and managed, "See ya."

3

Soon a few weeks had passed. Katie drifted through her school routine with difficulty. It felt so unreal. The world didn't seem to know that Ty had died. Her teachers compassionately allowed her extra time, but assignments still needed to be completed and she would still have to work hard to catch up. And now her older brother wasn't there to help her. When she had trouble with algebra, he used to give her great examples and helped her make sense of it. He would have been a great teacher, which was his dream, now unrealized.

Katie sat at her desk in her room and fought to concentrate on the math problems. It was about three o'clock in the afternoon and she and Alex would have the house to themselves for a couple of hours before Mom and Dad got home from work.

Katie normally relished the quiet time, but today nothing helped. She couldn't think clearly and couldn't grasp the concepts. She put the paper aside and leafed through her notebook for her next assignment. Should she try her report on China? She reached for the encyclopedia CD, tapped the button to open the drive on her computer and sighed. No, she did not have the energy to struggle with a report.

Katie stared at her desk and let out a long breath. She noticed the CD for *"Reality Twist"* peeking out from beneath her notebook. *"Reality Twist"* was a virtual reality game Alex had recently gotten for his birthday. "Alex," Katie sighed. He must have left it in her room after using her game system – the only system in the house that would run the game. Both Alex and Ty proclaimed the game awe-some, but Katie had not yet tried it.

She pulled the case loose, held it in her hand and studied the cover. Soldiers in armor, a king, a warrior, a princess, an archer woman and some other characters all decorated the cover. In the background, a huge dragon spread its bat-like wings. It intrigued Katie.

Katie rolled the chair back from her desk and, still holding the case in her hand, walked to the end of her bed. She sat on her com-forter, across from her TV, leaned down and placed the disc into the game system's drive. She switched on the television and, as the screen flickered with light, she wondered what she was doing. Should she play a *game?*

The screen became clear, and large yellow letters on a black background slowly came into view and spelled *Reality Twist.* A swell of overpowering music filled Katie's ears and caused the hair on the back of her neck to rise. Smooth violins, the mellow tones of a French horn, the low vibrations of a cello, and the light, airy flirting of a flute merged together into a powerful melody. Shivers trickled up Katie's spine.

How could such grand music emit from the tiny speakers of her TV? The tones seemed so full, so real, so alive — as if she sat with the orchestra, and the musicians surrounded her.

The volume lowered softly, and the game title slowly faded out of view. Then a message was displayed in yellow letters: "Place mask over eyes and gloves on hands."

Katie blinked. She almost felt like doing what it said. Would it be okay? What had the minister said at the funeral?

"Celebrate his life," the minister had declared. "Remember what he enjoyed and hold onto those memories."

Ty had loved virtual reality games and he had especially enjoyed this game. Could she allow herself a little diversion — in memory of Ty?

Katie found one of the masks amid papers on the floor by her desk, and near it sat one pair of the gloves. She lifted the mask with her right hand and slowly studied its shape. The solid plastic fit over the player's eyes like a smooth goggle and extended over the player's ears. She picked the gloves up from the pile of papers with her left hand. They contained tiny silvery threads and small plates that looked like electronic chips. Katie quickly wiggled her fingers into them; they felt warm and comfortable. She paused. The monitor still displayed "Place mask over eyes and gloves on hands." Her heartbeat quickened and Katie's mouth turned dry. She positioned the mask over her eyes and ears.

Wondrous music filled her head. Ahead of Katie, in bright yellow, the words "Choose Player" appeared floating in the air over a black background. She raised her right hand and a fake-looking, computer-generated arm appeared. She pointed her blocky finger and touched the option to select her character.

The area in front of her changed. A white-bordered frame appeared and inside it stood a tall man. He had blond hair and wore a rough, cloth vest and coarse pants – almost like burlap – and he held a large sword. Katie thought this character looked like a barbarian warrior. His name, "Oxtis," appeared beneath the frame. Oxtis' frame retreated and sat in the upper left-hand corner of the screen. What character had Ty chosen when he played? If he had talked about it, she could not remember.

Next, a female character appeared in view. A tall, pointed hat adorned her head, and a floating pink scarf draped down from the hat's tip. She wore a silky pink dress and looked like a princess. Her name was "Sareeta." Katie did not want to be a princess. She curled her lip and felt the mask push up on her cheeks. She waited and more frames appeared in front of her.

The fifth character, a woman with short brown hair, stood proudly. She looked to be in her late twenties and had a mature, feminine figure. The character had wide-set, brown eyes, a medium-sized nose, smooth cheeks and a strong chin. She wore calf-length pants and a short-sleeved tunic made of brown cloth with a delicate weave. On her feet she wore black leather boots with crisscrossed lacing up the front. A thick black belt encircled her waist. Strapped to her left forearm was a small crossbow, and wrapped around her forefinger was the trigger string. The edge of a quiver and the tails of feather-tipped arrows appeared over her left shoulder and the quiver strap crossed her chest. This character's name was "Aknia." She looked strong and confident and that appealed to Katie. She wished she could be that way, wished she could face anything without fear, instead of being insecure and withdrawn. Katie raised her computer-generated arm again and touched the frame of Aknia's picture. The white outline brightened, stayed in the center of the screen, and the remaining characters dissolved into blackness.

Over the picture of Aknia, the words "Choose Weapons" appeared. Katie reached up and selected this option. Aknia's frame remained in the background, as rows of small white rectangles came into view. Within each rectangle, a weapon of some kind was displayed; one showed a large sword, another showed a small knife. Unsure what kind of weapons would be useful in this imaginary world, Katie did not select anything. She touched the word "End" which appeared in the lower left-hand corner of the screen.

Next, "Choose World" appeared over the image of Aknia. Katie raised her arm once again and pointed to the words. A series of white-bordered frames emerged. The first box showed the interior of an old stone castle with torchlight flickering on the gray walls. The second frame displayed a grassy hill with snow-peaked mountains in the background. A breeze flowed over the tall grasses, making the weeds flow in green waves. Katie loved the mountains so she immediately raised her computer arm and pointed to the second frame. The dark background behind Aknia changed to show the selected world.

The music, previously playing quietly in the background, swelled into Katie's ears, making her wince slightly, but also tingle with excitement. The image of Aknia, standing on the grassy hill, floated toward Katie.

A wave of dizziness swept over Katie. The grassy hillside drew in around her and enveloped her. Katie swayed slightly as she slowly realized she actually stood on the hill, and as she raised her arms up to steady herself, she stared in disbelief. *These aren't my pale arms — they're tanned!* Katie frowned, shocked. Her arms looked real, not fake or computer-generated at all. Freckles even dotted her skin and a breeze ruffled fine, light hairs on her right forearm. She felt the soft touch of the wind against her skin and a shiver of excitement raced through her. *Unbelievable!* She clenched and unclenched her fists. She did not feel the gloves at all; she only felt skin and fingers. She stared at her hands and blinked, suddenly aware that the mask no longer covered her face and eyes. She raised her hand to her face, touched her forehead and eyebrows and then once again studied her arms.

Attached to her left forearm was the crossbow. One strap circled near her elbow, the other near her wrist and appeared to be made of leather. She felt the weight of the crossbow press against her skin. Around her pointer finger she felt the tightness of the trigger string. She lowered her left arm, reached behind her with her right hand, and pulled an arrow from the quiver that rested on her back. The shaft felt rough, but the feathers soft. No wonder Ty and Alex loved this game so much. It made everything seem so real! Katie smiled to herself and replaced the arrow in the quiver.

With astonishment, Katie inhaled warm, fresh air into her lungs, felt the air flow through her nostrils and into her throat, and saw her chest rise and fall. The sun warmed her skin like a wool blanket. How could this be? She actually felt as though she stood on a hill in bright sunshine with gentle breezes passing over her. Katie held her new hands out. She wanted to touch the tall, waving grasses around her. The weeds — some with soft, caterpillar-shaped tips and some just tall, thick blades — tickled her outstretched palms. She inhaled deeply, completely awestruck. She wanted to see more of this world. What should she do now? Which way should she go?

To her right, down a hill, spread a forest dark with trees, some with boughs of long pine needles and some with leafy branches that waved and swayed in the breeze. Small green bushes grew in the shadow of the trees. To her left stretched a series of other forested slopes, each higher than the last. Beyond the slopes, off in the distance, rose snow-peaked mountains.

Down to her lower right, yellow letters displayed the words "Health 100%," "Food 0%," and "Weapons 33%," and seemed to float over the grasses. Only the presence of the words distracted her from the overwhelming reality of the game.

The dizziness passed. Katie tried to step to her left, toward the gradually rising slopes and snowy peaks. She grimaced with effort but her legs would not move. It seemed like other games — she could only move her character in a certain direction. Katie then turned to her right and stepped easily through the tall, waving grasses down the hill toward the forest.

Had she stood from the edge of her bed? Katie didn't remember doing so. Did she walk in her room and would she soon bump into the wall? Katie couldn't believe it, but she walked and walked and didn't slam into the wall. She felt dirt and stones under her feet — not carpet. She heard no dogs barking, heard no car engines roar or tires squeal. She felt as though she had been transported into this imaginary world and now existed in it as Aknia, the archer woman.

Katie thought that she was 6 or 7 inches taller now and she wished she could be as tall as this character in reality, but knew that she probably would never reach more than 5'3" or 5'4". She had inherited her stature from her mother instead of her father. Aside from her height, Aknia's arms and legs felt quite defined and powerful. Katie remembered feeling this fit herself, just before she quit gymnastics.

Katie walked down the hillside, her feet softly crushing the green blades against the brown dirt. Farther down the knoll, hard rocks and small stones poked against the thin soles of her boots. At the base of the slope, a small stream trickled and gurgled. It looked and sounded real. She leapt from one side of the creek to the other and landed with a slight thud, her strong, new legs bending with the impact. A small dirt cloud puffed up from the ground. Upon landing, Katie expelled air through her nose and partly opened mouth. She felt alive – like she really *had* jumped over the stream!

Ahead of her, halfway up the next hill, stretched the forest. She climbed, pressing her legs into the slope, and entered the woods. The air turned noticeably cooler as she stepped into the shadow of the trees. She smelled the tangy pine. Fallen, dry pine needles and crispy leaves crunched under her footfalls.

Katie had never played this game before and did not know the objective. How did you win? Were there creatures in the forest that she would have to defeat in order to advance from level to level? She did not know. For the moment she only enjoyed the reality of being away from her room, away from responsibilities and far, far away from grief.

The forest became denser and darker as Katie hiked along. She pushed branches away from her face and body with effort. As she continued through the woods, Katie felt an eerie sensation and she slowed down and cautiously continued forward. She felt as if something was watching her. Did something lurk up ahead ready to pounce? She halted and reached behind her back, pulled an arrow out of the quiver, placed it on the crossbow and pulled the drawstring back, locking the shaft into place. If she squeezed her pointer finger toward the palm of her hand, the arrow would spring from the crossbow.

Katie scanned the leaves and listened to the wind. It sounded like a whisper. Or was it words? She could barely distinguish them until they drew nearer and formed into recognizable tones and she heard the light breath ask, *"Who are you?"*

Katie's breathing quickened, but she did not respond. She scanned the leaves and branches for someone but saw nothing except the waving of the boughs in the breeze. She heard small scurries and the rustle of leaves. Was something or someone approaching? Afraid to move and afraid to speak, she stayed still and silent, waiting for the next sounds. She heard nothing except a few chirps and cheeps from birds.

Thinking it safe to move on, she lifted her right leg but then wavered as her foot tugged on something. The archer looked down and placed her right foot back on the ground. A leafy vine had wrapped around her ankle. She tried to pull away from its grasp, but it gripped tighter. Swiftly, from the trees around her, more vines extended, reaching, crackling and twisting quickly around her arms and legs. They restrained her so fast! She tried to pull free but her struggling made them tighten.

The tendrils yanked her legs out from under her, and she fell on her back on the ground, her breath briefly knocked out of her. Dull pain from the impact flared as she coughed and gasped. From the corner of her eye she noticed the "Health" reading drop from 100 percent down to 95. She cursed herself for not paying attention when she'd started the game. Where was the option to exit?

She struggled against the grip of the twines, shifting her shoulders, arms and legs as more vines wriggled around her, covering her chest. They began to squeeze and compress, pressing the air from her lungs. She gasped. Her chest seared with pain. Her lungs burned like fire! She saw the health meter drop down until it reached 50 percent.

Katie wanted desperately to reach up and remove the mask from her face and break this game's grip on her, but the vines pinned her arms to her sides. She relaxed, thinking that possibly they would loosen if she did not fight; however, more vines extended and swished around her, creating a cocoon of tendrils and leaves.

Katie's heart pounded in her head and she gasped for breath as the vines wrapped around her face covering her eyes and ears, then covering her mouth. What would happen? Would she simply run out of health and then the game would stop? But the pain felt so real! She inhaled again, her lungs filled only with stinging stabs as she struggled for breath. It shouldn't feel like this! Her vision slowly became peppered with dots of black. The health meter dropped to 30 percent and kept dropping – 20 percent, 10 percent. And just before the meter displayed 0, she distinctly heard a voice whisper, *"Katie."*

In darkness and terror, Katie floated up and back, now free of the vines and able to breathe. She felt as though the world flowed around her and it caused a queasy feeling to sweep over her. Then she stood in a black room, and large yellow letters in front of her displayed the words, "Game Over."

Katie quickly pulled the mask from her eyes and the gloves from her fingers. Her head pounded and her stomach swayed. But she felt certain that someone had said her name! Was that part of the game? Or had she imagined it? Trembling with fear and panic, Katie tried to calm herself down. But she felt so sick. She wavered, feeling faint, and dropped back onto her quilted comforter. She closed her eyes and wished that the room would quit spinning.

Katie awoke and realized that she must have fallen asleep – or passed out. Darkness filled her room except for light rays from the hallway peeking in under her door. What time was it? She sat up, raised her left hand to her pounding head and looked at her glowing clock on the nightstand; it read six o'clock. Hours had passed.

Katie shakily stood up and walked across the floor to her door. She opened it and stepped into the hallway. She felt so weak she could barely walk and used the walls to guide her toward the bathroom. Once there, she pulled open the medicine cabinet and grasped a bottle of Tylenol.

"There you are," Audry sighed from the hall.

Katie jerked and turned to face her mother, who stood in the doorway. Audry's face showed concern and she reached out for Katie and said, "I thought I'd let you sleep, but are you all right?"

"I don't feel very good," Katie said, shaking her head. "I have a terrible headache and I feel like I'm going to throw up." Should she tell her mother that the virtual reality game had made her sick? Should she tell her that she had been playing a *game*?

Audry placed the outside of her hand on Katie's cheeks. "I don't think you have a fever," Audry said. She helped Katie get the lid off the bottle and take two of the pills.

"Do you want some soup or something?" Audry asked after Katie had swallowed a gulp of water with the two capsules.

"No. I just want to go back to bed," Katie said. She hugged her mom and then stumbled back to her bedroom.

Katie flopped onto her bed and rolled onto her back. A voice in the game had spoken her name. No, it couldn't be. She tried to remember if one of the other character's names was "Katie." She felt sure none had her name. Had it been her imagination? Who would have called to her from a virtual world? Katie wondered beyond all sense and reason if the ghostly, bodiless voice could have been Ty.

4

Around noon the following day, Katie rushed from geography class down the crowded school hallways. She clutched her books to her chest and slipped her small frame past a group of seniors who whispered as she passed. Their murmurs irritated Katie. She wanted desperately to scream at them, "Yes! It was my brother who died — now leave me alone!" However, she kept her silence and swiftly walked toward the commons.

Katie couldn't wait for lunch, couldn't wait to talk with Jessie. She wanted to tell Jessie — tell her what? That a voice had called her name in a virtual reality game? No, Katie decided, regaining her senses, she would tell Jessie nothing.

Katie grabbed a sandwich, chips and a pop, and wound her way through the congested, noisy tables toward the place where she, Jessie and a few others usually sat.

Jessie looked up and smiled gently as Katie stepped closer. That smile meant so much to Katie. Jessie had been so understanding during the last few weeks. She had offered her shoulder for tears and support several times. Jessie had been so kind and brave, and yet Katie knew it must be difficult for Jessie as well. They had known each other since the third grade and Jessie, an only child, had spent most of her free time with the Martin kids. Katie knew she could confide in Jessie, but wondered what her best friend would think if she told her about the game. Katie studied Jessie's greenish-brown eyes, and Jessie's brows slowly pressed together as she frowned.

"Are you okay?" Jessie asked, reaching for Katie's right arm.

Katie realized that she had been staring at Jessie, and she shook her head, breaking her trance, and stammered, "I'm fine. I'm okay."

"Are you sure?" Jessie prodded. "You looked like you wanted to tell me something."

Katie sat down heavily and placed her food and books on the table. Jessie could read Katie's expressions better than anybody, and Katie knew she could hide nothing from her, but it wasn't right. She couldn't tell her, not yet. "No. Just thinking," Katie managed.

Jessie nodded compassionately and let Katie be. Katie ate her lunch quietly. At the end of their lunch break, when the electronic bell sounded, they said good-bye and went on to their remaining classes.

That evening, Katie sat at the dinner table with Alex to her right. Dad sat at the left end of the oak dining table and Mom sat at the opposite end. And across from Katie sat an empty chair – Ty's chair. Alex would not sit there and neither would Katie. It was Ty's place, and even though he would never sit there again, neither Katie nor Alex would move to the other side of the table.

Audry asked how school was and Alex and Katie both responded that it was fine. Katie marveled at how ordinary conversations seemed extraordinarily forced and awkward since they had experienced their loss. Perhaps it was because the one thing they all wanted to talk about remained silently forbidden, because to speak of him would cause too much pain.

Sam cleared his throat, and Katie expectantly looked up from her mashed potatoes. Sam took a few short breaths and then said, "Katie." He would not look Katie in the eye and simply stared at the table. "I want you to give me your car keys."

Katie could not believe what he had just said. She searched his profile for an explanation, but he would not look at her. Katie turned to look at her mother, but Audry did not raise her eyes from her plate. The way Mom acted, it was as if she were in silent agreement with Dad. What was wrong with them?

"Give me your car keys," Sam ordered again.

He didn't have to say why, Katie knew why — because of Ty's accident.

"But Dad, I…I'll be careful." Katie pleaded, but stopped because immediately after she said it, she realized she had implied that Ty had not been careful and she did not want to malign Ty.

Sam did not look up and simply raised his right palm and pronounced, "There will be no discussion. Just give me your keys."

Exasperated, Katie took a few short breaths and glanced from her dad to her mom. She noticed Alex stared down at his peas, pretending he didn't hear anything.

She could not argue with Dad because, if he wanted to, he could just take the keys out of her purse. He could even disable her car so that she couldn't drive. Apparently he didn't want to do either — just wanted to force Katie to relinquish her keys. He had all the power and Katie had none. Tears of frustration began to form and Katie, embarrassed to be crying for this reason, got up quickly from the table and walked into the den and over to her purse. She sniffed quietly, searched in the front pocket for her red key ring, and when she found it, clenched her fingers around it and held it to her chest. She tried to control her emotions; she didn't want to bawl in front of them over this, not after losing Ty.

Katie walked back to the table and stood by her father's side. "Dad, I promise I'll…."

"Katie, give me your car keys," Sam said through tight lips.

Tears pooled at the base of her eyes. Filled with anger, frustration and sadness, Katie shoved her keys into his palm, then she turned away and raced up the stairs to her room.

Katie slammed the door shut and threw herself onto her bed. It was so unfair! Yes, Ty had an accident. That didn't mean that she was destined to as well! She was a careful driver and would *never* lose control of her car. Yet even as she thought it, she knew Ty had never intended to lose control of his car either. The road was icy and somehow it had happened. *Somehow* it happened, so why should she give up her privileges because he had made a mistake! Yes, the perfect Ty had made a mistake. The flawless, wonderful boy who could do no wrong! What was she thinking? The sudden bitterness and hatred she felt frightened her. She didn't want to think it. There was no place for this anger in her grief.

Tears dropped down her cheeks and then Katie felt extremely guilty. She cried for herself and not for Ty. It felt wrong. But why shouldn't she cry for herself? Dad had taken away her car keys! So she lay on her bed and cried silently, muffling her sobs in her pillow. Finally, after half an hour, she pulled the tear-soaked cloth away from her face and dialed Jessie.

The tones of the phone ringing on the other end pulsed into Katie's ear. What would she say to Jessie? Would she sound stupid and childish to complain about what her father had done?

"Hello?" Jessie's mom answered the phone.

"Hi, Mrs. Holden. Is Jessie there?" Katie tried to keep her voice from quavering but failed.

"Yes, Katie," Mrs. Holden affirmed gently. "Just a sec."

Katie wondered how she should tell Jessie. Should she rant about how mad she was at her parents right now? What would Jessie think of her? Or should she just simply ask her friend if it could be her turn to drive to school in the morning?

"Katie? How are you?" Jessie spoke hesitantly.

"Jessie," Katie said, fighting her twitching chin. "My dad took my car keys away from me."

"He did what?" Jessie exclaimed.

"Took my keys away." Katie trembled with anger. "Can you believe it? I'm so angry right now! But," Katie hesitated, "do you think that's horrible of me? To be so mad about what my dad did?"

"No, I don't think that's horrible." Jessie supported her. "I'd be mad. But you know why he did it."

"Yeah. He doesn't want me to have an accident like…." Katie stopped. She closed her eyes and grimaced. She wouldn't say it.

"Well, maybe he just wants to keep you from driving until spring when the weather gets better. Did you ask him?" Jessie continued.

"I couldn't. I was so mad I couldn't say anything." Katie sighed. "Do I sound selfish? I mean, do I sound stupid? Ty's gone and here I am whining over having my car keys taken away."

"No. Don't think that way, Katie. It's okay. It'll be okay. Let it go for a couple of months and then ask him if you can have them back."

Understanding Jessie. Wise Jessie. So calm and so reserved, yet she always seemed to know the right thing to say. Katie always felt awkward and struggled to find the right words. She felt like a lot of the time she just let things fall out of her mouth.

"I know he's hurting terribly and so is Mom, but so am I, and Alex, too. I just don't understand – but I do. Does that make sense?" Katie sighed.

"Of course it does," Jessie assured her calmly.

Katie smiled and relaxed. She did not feel embarrassed any more. Jessie could make it all better.

After a short pause Jessie spoke. "You know what's funny?"

"What?" Katie sighed.

"Ty would be the one to talk your parents into letting you drive again," Jessie stated.

Katie knew it was true and it hurt. After her little mishap running over the trash can, hadn't he convinced their parents that it was okay for Katie to continue driving?

"You're right. He would have. God, I miss him." Katie massaged her temples.

"I miss him, too," Jessie said.

Katie felt sure her friend missed Ty in ways she had not put into words. Both fell silent. Katie swallowed hard, feeling morose. Jessie grieved as well, but Katie did not know what to say and fought back tears.

Then Jessie said, "I'll pick you up tomorrow. Don't worry about it. Next week was going to be my turn anyway."

"Okay," Katie sighed. They were quiet again for a few seconds and then Katie said, "Jessie?"

"Yeah?" Jessie responded quietly.

Would this be a good time to tell her friend about the game? About hearing the voice? And about wondering if it could possibly be Ty? No. Not a good time Katie decided and simply breathed, "Thanks."

"See ya tomorrow," Jessie said.

Katie hung up the phone and hoped that Jessie didn't think her behavior odd. She hoped, and knew, that Jessie would forgive her awkwardness and selfishness. And Jessie was right, Ty would have defended her. Katie missed him, and she found herself wondering if *he* had called her name. Katie *had* to find out.

Katie could not believe her own actions. She loaded the game into the system, tugged the gloves over her hands and placed the mask on her face. The music tingled up her spine and the familiar characters appeared.

Again she chose Aknia. When prompted to select a weapon, she touched the frame for the small knife. She thought it would allow her to cut through the vines and remain in the game longer; then she might be able to find out who had spoken to her. A sheath containing the small blade appeared, looped through the leather belt at Aknia's waist. Again she chose the grassy hill as her world, and Aknia's frame moved in toward Katie.

The world hugged her like a long lost friend. It embraced her and greeted her with its warmth. Katie found herself in sunlight, standing atop the grassy hill. The sounds of breezes and distant chirping birds filled her ears. She heard no airplanes, no helicopters. In fact that seemed silly; those types of machines didn't exist in this world. Katie lifted her chin, closed her eyes, and inhaled a long, deep breath of the fresh air.

I'm here, she thought and she hoped the voice would speak again. Katie tried to sense a presence but felt nothing. The archer then lowered her chin and opened her eyes.

This game felt so real! It gave her the sensation of being *in* the game, of breathing within the character's body, of seeing out of the character's eyes, of feeling with the character's hands. No wonder Ty loved it. Could that be why he was here? Was it his voice she had heard?

Katie stepped down the side of the grassy hill, leaped over the small, trickling stream and entered the forest. The archer drew the small knife from the sheath at her waist and held the blade ahead of her, in her right hand, ready to fend off the vines. She stepped through the brush and into the thickening woods. The archer remembered exactly the way the branches had looked just before the vine had grabbed her ankle. She watched her feet carefully, waiting for the first tendril to reach out and grasp her. As the first green leaves wriggled through the edge of the forest toward her, Katie stiffened and swept her small blade down toward the vine. Got it! She severed a few inches and the piece dropped to the ground, lifeless. The remaining leafy twine streaked back into the bushes. A light-green fluid seeped out of the severed end and trailed along the pine needles and leaves that covered the dirt. She heard more rustlings, and more vines extended out of the trees and bushes around her. She chopped the ends off, and the light-green goo dripped down over the forest floor.

She ran and seemed to be escaping the vines when her foot slipped down a muddy slope and into a marshy pond. Katie lost her balance and sloshed into the mush, sinking quickly. She reached up and grasped overhanging branches and tried to pull herself up out of the muck. The mud clung to her, reluctant to release her legs. She fought and strained, reaching for a higher limb. Suction from the mud slipped the boot from her right foot, and the marsh finally released her. She hung from the branches and looked around. Vines encroached on the marshy pond and up into the trees. She would have to climb across to the other side, or exit the game.

She had so hastily jumped back into the game that she had forgotten to check for an option to exit. She quickly looked down, but only the displays for food, weapons and health glowed below. With her knees hooked over a branch and her left arm steadying herself, Katie reached for her face and tried to pull off the mask, but felt only Aknia's eyes, forehead and ears. How could she get out? Katie realized she'd gotten herself stuck in this game, and it maddened and frustrated her. She would have to keep playing.

Vines began to grow thick around her and, with her heart beating faster, she tried to propel herself quickly through the branches. Katie swung shakily from limb to limb, but could not outrun the vines. They quickly encased her and she gasped for air. Katie held her breath as the foliage folded in around her body and face, and she frantically kicked to try to work herself free. The vines once again had her in their grip! She saw her health meter drop down to 10 percent and knew the inevitable approached. She struggled to hold onto her last gasp of air, but soon felt herself losing consciousness.

Katie felt ill, heavy and dizzy. Then she found herself standing in the black room. In front of her, large yellow letters displayed the words, "Game Over." She snatched the mask off her face and dropped it to the floor. She collapsed to her knees, breathing heavily and stared down at the thing. Then Katie pulled the gloves from her hands and tossed them to the carpet. This game was too real. Too weird.

A droplet of sweat formed at her temple and slid down her cheek. She trembled and quivered. Shakily, she walked across the carpeted floor, out into the hallway and down to the bathroom. Katie splashed her sweaty face with cool water and stared at her pale, thin features in the mirror.

Her own blue eyes stared back at her and she smoothed her hair down. Katie wondered what was going on in her mind. Was she losing all touch with reality? She studied herself in the mirror, then patted her skin dry, and felt normalcy creep shakily back to her. She brushed her teeth – and avoided looking at Ty's toothbrush. Then she went back to her room.

Katie crawled into bed and tried to sleep. She tossed like the thoughts in her mind. Was it really him or had she just imagined it? Her mind had tricked her before. She remembered the dream, when she had seen Ty in her doorway. Was it a dream? Or was it his ghost, his spirit? Was he trying to reach out to her somehow through the game? What a *crazy thought!*

But she *knew* she had heard it. There was a clear difference between hearing your own little voice in your head and hearing someone speak. She felt certain she had heard someone say her name. But it was just a game!

Katie gripped her face in her hands and shivered. She breathed deeply and tried to clear her head because this was making her nuts.

Finally, she relaxed and felt heavier and heavier. Maybe soon she would drop off to sleep.

5

At school the next day, Katie sat in math class and daydreamed about *"Reality Twist."* It was 8:50 a.m., and Mr. Morris droned on about math problems. Katie heard nothing of what he said. She stared out the glass-paned windows, wishing the day was over and thought, *Maybe I need to go farther in order to see who it is.*

Katie wondered if she needed some other weapon or tool in order to get past the marsh. She remembered seeing a grappling hook and rope displayed as one of the weapons, and decided she would choose them the next time she played. She could toss the hook above her head and into the branches and, when it held, she could swing across the bog and away from the vines.

She tried to listen to Mr. Morris. What did he say? Math was already enough of a challenge for her. She needed to pay attention, but her thoughts kept drifting toward the game.

She imagined herself traveling through the forest again and felt a strange weight against her left forearm. She jerked awake from her daydream and touched her skin. For a moment, she felt as if the crossbow had been strapped to her arm. Katie quickly looked around. Had anyone noticed her twitch? No, everyone just sat in their chairs listening to Mr. Morris. She relaxed. Thank goodness no one had seen her jump.

Katie meandered through the rest of the school day. After her final class, she went back to her locker and grabbed the books she would need to complete her homework. Then she walked out to

Jessie's car. She stood by the passenger side in the brisk wind and shivered in her purple coat. A small bit of snow still coated the parking lot and the cold crept up through the soles of her tennis shoes, chilling her feet.

A few moments later, Jessie walked up to the driver's side. "I didn't think today would ever end!" she declared as she unlocked the doors.

Katie simply nodded in agreement and got into the car. Katie rode home from school quietly, deep in thought.

Compassionately, Jessie finally asked, "Do you want to talk about it?"

Katie jerked out of her silence and stared at Jessie. Did she want to talk about it? Yes, she did. Desperately in fact, but would Jessie believe her? Or would Jessie think she had gone over the edge, off the deep end, lost a few marbles or the whole bag?

"No," Katie said, shaking her head and lowering her chin to her chest.

"Okay," Jessie responded and nodded.

Jessie turned the corner and pulled up in front of Katie's house. Katie opened the car door and got out, but before she closed the door, she saw Jessie lean across the passenger seat and peek up at her.

"If you do want to talk, just call me. Okay?" Jessie said.

Katie bit her lower lip and nodded her head. She went inside the house, shed her coat and quickly sped up to her room, carrying her backpack. Alex would not be home for a few minutes, and Mom and Dad would be at work for a couple more hours. Should she play the game or do her homework? She had a lot of homework, so she reluctantly turned on her computer and dropped her pack to the floor.

What should she work on first? Did it really matter? Her grades were slipping. Let them fall. She really didn't care, but she knew she should. *Work hard in his memory,* she prodded herself. Get good grades like him because he would have wanted her to. She pulled her geography book out of her pack and plopped it open on the desk.

Ten minutes later, Katie heard the front door open and then slam shut. She heard her younger brother bound up the stairs and into the hallway. Then she heard a tentative knock on the door to her bedroom.

"Katie," Alex spoke as he rapped his knuckles on the wood. "Can I come in?"

"Sure," Katie said and she turned as he pushed open the door. "What's up?" she asked. She had felt so sorry for Alex through all of this. He had changed so drastically. He used to be a pain, a total imp; he would do things just to bother her. But he had become quiet, and actually nice, tolerable. Katie knew it hurt him terribly to lose his older brother.

"I was wondering if I could have my game back," Alex said pointing to the case that held *Reality Twist.*

"Oh," Katie said as she reluctantly reached for the case on her desk. She didn't want to let him have it. She wanted to keep it for herself. What was she thinking? It was just a game, wasn't it?

"You can play," Katie told him, acting nonchalant. She motioned to the game system, picked up a mask and a pair of gloves from her floor, and handed them to Alex. She wanted to watch his actions. She wanted to know how she could walk such great distances and never run into anything.

"Okay." Alex nodded, somewhat suspicious.

Alex sat on the end of Katie's bed and slipped the disc into the tray. Katie anxiously watched her brother put on the gloves and mask. She breathed shallowly, with anticipation. The music would be playing now. Did it make his spine tingle the way it had hers?

He raised his arm and she knew he would be choosing a character and her heart thumped. Which one did he choose? She watched intently as he moved his arm again, picking a weapon, and then one more time, selecting his world.

Then he stood and planted his feet squarely. He held fisted hands up in front of him, one atop the other, as if he gripped an invisible sword. He swished his arms from side to side and grunted and groaned with effort. He backed up, nudged the end of her bed and slightly lost his balance. Then he took a large step to his right and bumped into the edge of her desk and backed away. Katie frowned as she watched him. He kept running into things. She had hiked over the hilltop and down into the forest without hitting anything.

Alex jabbed his fists forward and back, out to his left and then to his right. She wondered what he fought against. He delivered a final parry, jerked as if something had startled him, then touched the air to his lower left as if he were selecting the option to end. Then he slowly removed the mask and gloves and placed them on the TV. He looked a little frightened, but he tried to hide it.

He turned toward Katie with an expression of guilt. "I know it seems wrong to play, but it reminds me of him."

"That's okay," Katie assured Alex. "I've played it myself."

"You have?" Alex frowned and then smiled. "It is *so cool,* isn't it? It seems so real!" His brown eyes shone bright with a light she hadn't seen in them for weeks.

"I know," Katie agreed with him. "It is *so* awesome. I can feel the sun on my skin and the breeze in my hair." She raised her hand to her hair and lowered it slowly when she saw Alex's brows scrunch. He looked confused. Why would that mystify him? He must have felt it as well. Should she ask him if he ever heard a voice?

"When you play," Katie hesitated, scared of what he might think if she asked about a voice, and then continued, "What world do you choose?"

"I like the castle. There are soldiers and stuff." Alex smiled with excitement.

The castle. Katie imagined what it would feel like in the game, being in that frigid, stone building, and asked, "Is it cold in there?"

Alex frowned again and smirked. "No." He shook his head and blinked at her, as if he couldn't believe what she had just asked.

Katie waved her hand feeling suddenly foolish and worried that he thought she was nuts. "I mean that it is so intense that you *almost* feel like you're warm or cold," she lied.

Alex nodded with relief and then shrugged. "Well, I guess I better get some homework done," Alex said and quickly exited Katie's room before she could ask him any more questions.

Maybe the game only felt real to her and not to anyone else. Katie felt sure she hadn't imagined the warmth of the sun. It was as if she had actually been standing under its rays out on that hilltop. When she had passed into the shade of the trees, her skin *had* felt cooler, as if she really *had* walked into the shadows.

She suddenly wondered if the castle would feel real too. Without hesitation she put on the mask and gloves again and entered the game. She chose Aknia, the archer woman, as her character, but — curious about the castle, and wondering if it did feel cold — she selected the citadel as her world.

The frame of Aknia, with gray stone behind her, moved toward Katie. Dizziness swept over her. She felt pressure all around her body, as if the castle pressed in around her. She blinked slowly. She stood in a corridor. Torches sputtered as they sat in iron brackets affixed to the gray stone walls around her. She heard the slight flutter of the torch's flames. She pressed her right arm out to steady herself and felt the smooth stone chill the palm of her hand. She shook her head and breathed in the cool, musty air of the old castle. It *was* cold. Did Alex just not feel it?

The archer walked down the corridor. Her boots made light scrapes as she stepped down the passageway. Sparsely placed torches flickered and sputtered. Katie smiled to herself as she passed a torch and felt heat radiate from the flame.

An end to the hallway appeared ahead of her, with an opening to the right. Alex had said there were soldiers. Were the soldiers bad guys? When Alex played, had he fought them, or some other creature? Katie did not know what might appear around the corner. She loaded the crossbow, stepped more cautiously and slowly toward the archway, and quickly extended her head out around the corner. She did not see anything. No soldiers appeared in this passageway. She stepped to the right and continued down the next corridor.

Another junction appeared, this time with openings to both the left and right. She advanced carefully up to the intersection, slipping her right foot across the stone and sliding her left foot up behind, then waited, wondering if something would strike from either side. She looked both left and right quickly, watching for any motion, any shadow crossing the walls. Nothing. She advanced another step and snatched a peek down each corridor. Both sides were empty.

The archer then proceeded to the left. Only the soft touch of her boots and the sputter of the torches echoed lightly in the hallway. As she walked along, she noticed a wooden door on her left. She stopped in front of the door and tried the latch with her right hand. The door did not open. She looked at the knob and saw a lock. She must need a key to open the door. What or who was behind the door, and where would she find a key?

She began walking down the long corridor again and saw a shape on the floor, to her left. Was it a key? No, it did not glint, and as she drew nearer the shape began to look like a brown, cloth sack. When she stood over it, she reached down, picked up the sack and opened it. Inside were small blocks of pale yellow cheese and a couple of round loaves of bread. Katie noticed that her food display, on the lower right, switched from 0 to 100 percent. She wondered if the food would have a taste.

Katie eagerly reached into the sack and grabbed a hunk of cheese. The archer bit off a piece and tasted its mellow flavor. Her mouth even salivated as she chewed the chunk. She swallowed and then pulled a toasted crust off the edge of the brown loaf and crunched it in her mouth. She could actually taste the food! Katie shook her head, tucked the sack up tightly under her belt and continued down the hallway.

As she reached the end of the passageway, the corridor stopped and again splintered into two halls, one on the left and another on the right. Not knowing what might jump out at her, the archer approached the juncture cautiously. She held her crossbow ready and took each step carefully, furtively glancing from side to side. Again, she didn't see anything in the left or right corridors.

Katie decided to go down the right side this time. She turned, and immediately heard a grinding rumble. The floor under her feet vibrated. She quickly looked behind her and found that the entryway had been sealed off. Katie turned forward – the hallway ahead had been sealed as well! She was trapped! And the walls that closed off the corridor moved menacingly closer and closer to Katie.

Fear flashed through Katie and she breathed in short bursts. Her weapons were useless against the heavy stone! She searched around for anything with which to prop up the walls. The stone wall ahead of her scraped over two brackets, one on either side. Twisting iron screamed and the torches dropped to the floor as the grinding wall consumed the metal. Light from the fallen torch fluttered up from the ground, casting strange shadows onto the slowly moving stone.

Katie breathed quick, panicked breaths. What should she do? What could she do? Only inches away now, the walls ground and crunched closer and closer to Katie. The archer backed up against the wall and caught her breath as she felt it push her toward the opposite side. She pressed her useless arms against the stone as it sandwiched her. Horrible fear rose within Katie as the walls pressed in closer, snuffing out the torches.

She felt the walls begin to crush the air from her chest, glanced to her right and saw her health meter drop rapidly. Katie stared at the health meter, wishing that the crushing pain would end soon. The display showed 10 percent. Katie cried out, and as she felt consciousness leaving the Aknia character, the meter displayed 0.

Once again in the black room, she saw the large yellow words, "Game Over." Katie whipped the mask from her face and the gloves from her hands. A wave of nausea flowed through her. Katie placed a hand against her stomach. She felt as if she *had* eaten some cheese and bread — and felt as if it would be coming up at any moment.

She raced down the hall and into the bathroom, and vomited into the toilet. Katie shook all over and a cold sweat glistened on her pale skin. She washed out her mouth and splashed cool water on her face. Then she trudged back to her bedroom and flopped onto her bed.

Katie closed her eyes and tried to force away the sick feeling. She wanted her head to quit pounding and wished her stomach would settle down. Why had she done it? Why had she played that game again?

Alex knocked on her door. "You okay?" He spoke through the wood. He pushed her door open and stepped into her room. Katie thought he must have heard her get sick, and she was suddenly angry about his new concern. A few weeks ago he would not have cared.

Exasperated, Katie sat up and said, "No, I am not okay. I just played that game again because I thought…." She blinked heavily, realizing she had said too much, and raised a hand to her head.

"Thought what?" Alex asked.

"I thought…I'm not sure what I thought." Katie held her face in her hands and shook her head. Then she removed her fingers and looked up at her little brother. "I heard a voice. It called me by my name. It said, 'Katie.'"

Alex looked at her, and Katie thought that he didn't look too surprised, which astonished her. He sat down next to her on her bed.

"I thought maybe it was a character's name, but there aren't any with my name," she said, and watched her brother warily for his reaction.

Alex said nothing. His eyes brightened, a small, understanding smile curved his lips and he nodded slowly.

"Do you believe me?" Katie asked hesitantly.

Alex took a deep breath, looked like he was going to speak but paused, took another deep breath and then nodded again saying, "Yeah, I do."

"Have you heard it?" Katie excitedly asked. "Have you heard the voice, too?"

"Just a few minutes ago, when I played, I heard someone say *my* name," Alex confided.

They sat in silence, but Katie's mind raced and all of her thoughts made no logical sense. Was it Ty? Impossible!

"Let's play again – both of us this time," Alex suggested.

Katie's stomach swayed. She dreaded being caught in vines or crushing walls, but the possibility of finding out who spoke to them was too enticing.

6

Alex grabbed an extra set of gloves and a mask and slipped them on. Katie quickly put on her gloves and slid the mask into place over her eyes and ears. Once again the impressive music surged through her body.

The game title floated into view and then faded away. Options Katie hadn't seen before appeared and displayed the words "Single Player" and "Multiple Players." Katie looked to her left and saw Alex in the form of a blocky, computer-generated shape. He reached up and touched the option for multiple players.

The words "Choose Player" appeared, and a frame came into view containing the image of the large barbarian, Oxtis. His blond, shoulder-length hair drifted in a breeze and he stared forward with bright blue eyes. Alex chose the brute warrior to be his character and the figure floated in front of Alex. Katie chuckled to herself. Did Alex dream of being large and strong? Was that why he selected Oxtis?

Katie selected Aknia again and the archer's frame hovered in front of her; then the "Choose Weapons" option was displayed.

"How many weapons can you get?" Katie asked, and she noticed that her voice sounded monotone and fake, like an automated voice.

"You get three total. The characters all come with one, and you can chose two more," Alex answered, and his voice also sounded unreal. "Oxtis comes with a sword," Alex said as he chose a helmet with a long metal piece over the nose, and a round wooden shield with metal bands. The helmet appeared on top of the warrior's head. He held the shield in his left hand, over his chest, and gripped his sword in his right hand.

Katie again selected the small knife. It was easy to carry and easy to use. Then she chose a grappling hook and rope for her second weapon. The knife and grappling hook appeared on either side of Aknia's waist, and the crossbow rested on the archer's left forearm. The weapons display, in Katie's lower right, now showed 100 percent.

At the "Choose World" prompt, Katie studied the four worlds she had not yet explored. In one of the frames, a crystal-clear lake sparkled. A breeze kicked up small white-capped waves, and she heard them lap up against the shoreline. Another world showed a snowy cave opening with glittering icicles. A cold wind howled and a blizzard swirled. In the next, a river rushed over large rocks and roared with foamy white water. The last showed a deep and rocky red canyon.

"I tried to find where the voice was coming from in the forest world and in the castle," Katie explained. "I got a 'Game Over' both times. Should we try another one?"

Alex studied the frames and then looked to Katie. "How about the lake?" he suggested.

"Okay," Katie agreed and she pressed the frame.

The lake world swarmed in around them. Katie instantly stood on the shore. To her right, the lake water glistened and twinkled. To her left, the sand extended a bit, then dissolved into hillsides covered with trees and bushes. The warm yellow sun glowed above them. Katie tipped her head up, lifting her face toward the sun. She squinted and raised her hand to shield her vision. She closed her eyes, lowered her arm and absorbed the warmth on her face. She breathed deeply and then looked around for Oxtis.

The tall warrior stood examining his hands. Then he flexed his muscles and seemed very impressed and pleased with his strength.

"Wow, it's *never* felt like *this* before!" Alex exclaimed in a deep rumbling voice and turned to the archer. He raised a hand to his throat and looked as if he could not believe the sound of his voice, so mature and deep – not his normal squeaky thirteen-year-old voice.

"When you played before, did you ever feel like you *became* the character?" Katie asked Alex, stepping closer to the huge warrior.

The barbarian held his arms out, eyes wide with awe, and then lowered his shoulders and took a couple of steps toward the lapping water. "No. It *never* felt like this before. This is all so *real*. I can't believe it." The warrior squatted down by the edge of the lake. He dipped his fingers into the water, shook them off and looked to Katie. "It's *cold*," he rumbled with amazement.

Katie suddenly looked down to her right and left. She only saw the meters for "Health," "Food" and "Weapons," and no option to exit.

"Try to reach for the mask and take it off, or pull the gloves off," Katie prodded.

Alex looked disappointed, but reached up toward his eyes, reluctant to grasp the mask and remove it. His fingers clinked against the metal helmet and he frowned as he realized he could not feel the mask over his eyes, and immediately he looked at his bare fingers.

The archer nodded. "Once you're in here, you can't feel the mask or gloves. It's like once it has you, it won't let you go. I've failed a couple of levels. How do you win?"

"There is a key in each world and there are six worlds. You have to get all the keys in order to win," Alex explained.

Katie wondered what Alex would think if he saw what he looked like. She herself felt odd speaking and moving like Aknia but thinking like herself, and that thought made Katie curious.

Katie stepped closer to the mirror waters of the lake. Did she dare look at her reflection? Would it disturb her to see Aknia's face staring back? Katie took a deep breath and looked down into the water. A mature young woman looked back, not a freckled sixteen-year-old. She raised her arm to her head and touched her short brown hair, moved her hand down to her face and touched her thin lips. *I'm moving and touching this skin, but it's not me I see.* An uncomfortable sensation swept through Katie. A feeling so intense, she almost felt as if she were coming out of her skin. She quickly looked up, away from her reflection. *Don't think about it. It is all fake anyway. But it feels so real!* Katie swallowed and desperately redirected her thoughts. She wondered which way they should go.

She tried to turn to the right and follow the shore but could not move in that direction. Just as it was in other worlds, the program would not let her move in certain directions. She turned to the left and easily stepped toward Alex. The warrior sheathed his sword, and with the shield grasped in his left hand, he nodded, ready to proceed.

"I guess we go this way." The archer pointed down the sandy beach behind the warrior.

The huge brute led the way and the archer followed. She felt soft sand and small pebbles through the thin boots covering her feet. Farther from the shore, the ground became rough and rocky, forming slopes that almost completely ringed the sparkling lake. On the steep slopes, Katie noticed different kinds of trees, some with small, soft needles – firs perhaps – and some with big, tri-tipped leaves – possibly maples. Small bushes grew among the trunks. A few birds called to each other and a squirrel chattered a warning as the warrior and archer passed.

As they walked along, Katie heard a hawk's piercing screech. She searched the sky for the bird. She saw the hawk, with its large wings extended wide as it circled lazily in the blue sky. A few white clouds floated in the heavens, beyond the bird of prey.

"I feel like we're really walking. I can't believe I haven't run into a wall," Alex spoke in the warrior's low voice.

"I know. It's like the real world doesn't even exist while we're in here. I wish I understood why," Katie said. "This game is so weird, but so cool."

Up ahead, the sound of rushing water became distinct. Alex and Katie approached the noise, stepping from small pebbles and sand to larger rocks and stones.

"What do you think that is? A waterfall?" Alex asked over his shoulder.

"Sounds like it to me," Katie agreed.

Katie stepped carefully over the larger stones and rough rocks, not wanting to twist her ankle or tumble into the cold lake water. The archer stopped and wavered on the tops of small boulders. To her left, the shore disappeared, as if the lake hung on the edge of a cliff. Ahead of her, the clear water flowed over the rim of the lake and down out of view. Katie carefully balanced and leaned out. How far down did it go? Rushing water tumbled over rocks, and then dropped several feet below. Across the top of the waterfall, where the lake spilled over the ledge, stretched a large, round log half as tall as the warrior.

Alex turned to look back at Katie. He seemed to be asking if he should go on. Katie shrugged. Alex tipped his head to the side, smirked and turned back toward the log. He cautiously climbed up onto the long tree trunk and Katie followed. She gripped a root, but a splinter stuck down beneath her fingernail on her right hand, and she cried out and yanked her hand back. A sharp pang throbbed in her finger as she picked the brown sliver from her skin. This game felt real in everything, warm sunshine, sparkling water and pain. Katie saw her health meter drop to 98 percent. Then the archer placed her hands carefully on the bark and wedged her foot into a crack. She pulled herself up to the top of the monstrous trunk.

The warrior bounced on the trunk, testing its strength. It stayed in place. He glanced back to Katie. The archer raised and lowered her shoulders and nodded, drawing down the corners of her mouth and raising her eyebrows. She did not know where they needed to go and she thought it must be safe to cross, if the log supported the bulky barbarian. "Go ahead," she urged the huge warrior.

Alex started across. The archer followed, stepping along the top of the log cautiously and carefully, watching her footing. When she looked down at her feet, she saw the flowing water under the trunk and it made her dizzy. She swayed and looked just beneath the log to the white spray and tumbling water below. It poured into a pool at the base of the falls. It rumbled and roiled, but beyond the pool, a clear river flowed away.

A loud crack sounded. Katie caught her breath, bent her knees and held her arms out to steady herself. She stood perfectly still. Alex stopped as well.

"Go back!" Katie shouted above the roar of the waterfall. She tried to step backwards, but her legs wouldn't move.

"I can't!" Alex shouted.

"I can't either!" Katie grumbled through gritted teeth. "I guess we have to go across." Thinking their combined weight had created the fracture, she said, "I'll stay here and wait until you get to the other side."

The archer didn't move. She breathed lightly and watched the heavy warrior carefully step across the creaking log. She kept her eyes on the brute so that she wouldn't stare down at the tumbling water and lose her balance.

The trunk split; a cracking gap appeared just as Alex hopped off the log to the rocks. Katie's eyes grew wide. A fall from the log was not a sensation she wished to experience. When she looked down to watch her footing, the rushing water flowing beneath the log made her dizzy again. She wavered, but steadied herself.

"Come on!" Alex yelled, and reached his hands out to her.

Katie's heart beat in her neck and ears. *Don't look at the falls, just look at the trunk.* She held her arms out away from her body, trying to balance as best she could. Then she fixed her eyes on the warrior, only looking down in fast flashes to make sure of her footing. The log creaked and moaned. She inched her way across, while her heartbeat pounded in her ears.

She approached the split in the log and as she stepped near it, the fracture grew with a soft crack. It expanded until the smaller piece severed from the trunk, and the log turned, throwing Katie off balance. Katie inhaled sharply and then dropped one leg on either side and rode the log like a horse as it shifted, rolling to the left and crunching to rest on the sharp rocks at Alex's feet. *Move, Katie,* she urged herself. With one shaking leg on either side of the tree trunk, Katie quickly scooted along.

She pressed her hands against the rough bark of the tree, pushed up and swung her legs forward. The trunk end ahead of her cracked once again. *Hurry! You're almost there!* The sharp rocks on which the log rested acted like an axe, splitting the wood apart. Panic flashed through Katie like a bolt of lightning.

The warrior stood with his arms outstretched, ready to help his sister.

"No, Alex!" Katie shouted and motioned irritably for the brute to back away from the edge.

"C'mon!" He yelled, motioning for her to hurry. He didn't retreat.

What was she thinking? This was not her skinny thirteen-year-old brother ahead of her; this was a huge, muscular brute! She raced for his hand, feeling the log split and crack beneath her. The trunk twisted, she extended her hand and felt Alex's grasp just as the massive log splintered and slipped off the rocks. The warrior gripped Katie's wrist tightly. She swung over the edge near the rushing water and watched the log topple off the rocks, crash against the boulders below and splinter into pieces. Katie cried out, thrashed, and tried to grasp the warrior's arm with her other hand.

"I've got you," Alex called to her. "Remember? I'm really strong now. Quit kicking and I'll pull you up."

Katie relaxed some and quit flailing her legs about. She felt the muscular warrior easily pull her up over the edge of the falls. After he lifted her to her feet, she quickly staggered across the rocks and stones away from the waterfall and plopped onto the grassy, sandy ground. The archer breathed heavily. They had made it. But what else would the game throw at them? New dangers? A key? The elusive voice?

Katie's legs had been doused with the freezing water as she hung over the side by the waterfall. She shivered with fright and cold.

"You okay?" Alex looked down at his sister.

"I just need to rest a minute," Katie said. She actually felt tired and exhausted, as if she had just crossed a splitting log. Would rest really make her feel better? She looked down to her right and saw her health meter had dropped to 87 percent.

"What does it read?" Alex asked nodding down toward her right.

"Eighty-seven percent," Katie told the warrior.

The barbarian glanced around them and said, "We need to find food and healing elixir."

"Healing elixir?" Katie asked as she stood up and brushed sand from her clothing.

Alex nodded as he scanned the area. "The elixir appears in a small blue bottle and the food appears in a burlap sack."

Katie nodded; she remembered the food she had found in the castle, but she had never seen any small blue bottles.

Alex and Katie hiked along the shoreline, searching rocks and bushes for food or elixir. In a few minutes, Katie's heartbeat no longer throbbed in her ears, and her breathing returned to normal. Her cloth pants dried in the warm sunshine and the chill in her bones faded.

Katie could not find bottles or sacks of food and she began to wonder if there were any. She also wondered where the key was. They had narrowly escaped the log and she felt very grateful her brother had been there to catch her; if he hadn't, she would have failed again. She desperately wanted to get a key and to be successful in a level. Did she wish this because of the voice? Yes, but more than that, Katie wondered if it wasn't just her stubbornness and need to always win. She did not want to see those words "Game Over" again.

Up ahead of them, the shore of the lake curved slightly and jutted out. At the tip of the small peninsula, a mass of wings fluttered. Katie narrowed her eyes. It looked like a group of butterflies. Alternately the wings flashed yellow and black, and as the two approached the fluttering things, they heard buzzing. Katie halted, sending a small cloud of dust up from her feet.

"They're bees," Katie whispered, pulling at the warrior to stop him. As the two stood still, the swarm shifted from its hovering spot and swooped as one directly toward them. Katie screamed and tried to turn and run away, but her legs would not move to the left or backwards. Alex ran toward the swarm but then turned sharply and ran into the lake. Water splashed up from his feet as he ran. He threw his shield out, and flung the helmet from his head. His sword's sheath kicked up from the lake's surface as he dived under.

Katie followed quickly, bounding into the cold water. The buzzing grew louder, but she did not look back to see how close the swarm had gotten. Once she had waded up to her waist, she dove under the surface. The shock of icy cold shot a stabbing pain through her body. She fought to keep from gasping and held her breath. She turned under the water, her ears filled with muffled sounds, her eyes frozen in their sockets, and stroked back up toward the surface. The crossbow slipped off her arm and drifted down toward the bottom of the lake. *Oh, no! Not the crossbow!* Katie tried to stroke down after it but she needed a breath, gave up and swam toward the surface. A sinking feeling drifted through her. She had lost one of her weapons. She popped up out of the water, full sound returning to her ears – including the buzzing of the bees.

She noticed that the insects hovered near the edge of the lake, but would not venture out over the ripples. Treading water, she turned, looking for Alex. The brute surfaced with a splash and a shiver.

"Now what?" The warrior's deep voice quivered with cold.

"They can't come over the water," Katie said as she motioned toward the swarm with her head. She looked around. "But we can't stay in here." The archer's chin trembled. "It's freezing!"

Katie searched the shoreline. They could not go back to the beach where they had stood because the insects might swarm after them again. The bees shifted back to their hovering place where the shore jutted out into the lake. On the other side, to the right of the small peninsula, the shoreline curved back into thick green trees that grew right up to the water's edge. Then the lakeshore extended back out from the trees and a sandy beach appeared again. They would need to swim across the cove to put safe distance, and water, between themselves and the bees.

"There," Katie said, pointing across the cove to the shore beyond. The barbarian looked to where she pointed and started swimming for the beach. The archer followed, kicking and slicing into the water with her frozen arms and legs, but she found swimming very difficult. Her numb limbs felt heavy and would not move quickly and her head ached. Her strokes seemed to only carry her a few inches at a time. *C'mon, Katie,* she told herself. *You can do it. You can swim. Don't think about how cold it is, just move your arms and legs!* Katie's breath quickened as she noticed that her health meter had dipped to 50 percent.

Katie took in a breath and swallowed hard. She kicked, forcing her frozen legs and arms to move. She pressed on, each stroke bringing her closer to the shore. The icy water lapped up onto her face and numbed her cheeks and lips. *I am so cold!* Katie's mind screamed.

She saw the brute's head bobbing up and down with each of his strokes. The stronger, larger warrior made quicker progress through the freezing water. He turned and saw Katie struggling and paddled back toward her.

"No!" Katie yelled at him. She wanted him to get out of the cold. She didn't want harm to come to her brother. "Go!" She ordered him to proceed toward the shore and he struck out again slicing with rapid strokes.

Frustration and exhaustion set in. *I feel like I'm getting nowhere!* Katie thought. She swam with great effort, gulping in cold lake water, sputtering and struggling. She kicked again, not willing to give up.

Katie saw the warrior finally reach the shore and pull himself up out of the water, dripping and shivering. She quickly glanced over to where the bees continued to hover, but they did not swarm over to attack him. Her plan would work – if only she could reach the shore!

"Just a little farther!" The warrior shouted encouragement.

The beach finally drew closer and Katie shifted her legs down, feeling for the rocky and sandy lake bottom with her pointed toes. With the next kick, the archer's foot struck the bottom of the lake. She stroked forward and both feet touched the steep bottom. She sputtered as she felt a tug on her right ankle. What was that? Something had grasped her, but then lost its grip as she kicked toward shore. Her heart jumped into her throat and she kicked again, but felt restrained by something now tightening around her calf.

Katie gasped just as something pulled her under the surface. Again her ears filled with cold, muffled sounds. She struggled, trying to twist out of the grip of whatever had snagged her. She desperately pulled up toward the surface as her lungs began to spasm and felt as if they would burst. Finally, the thing let go of her.

Katie popped up out of the water and shifted around looking for whatever had grabbed her. She frantically kicked and swam as fast as she could toward the shore.

She heard Alex shout, "Hurry!"

Spurred by his yell, Katie focused on the warrior and willed her numb limbs into action. As she drew nearer to the shore, she saw Alex become frozen with fear. She stopped and turned to look behind her as a large, greenish-gray lump broke the surface. Water fell away as a head rose up and round black eyes became visible on either side under bony brows.

Katie's eyes grew wide and she turned and splashed with new strength toward the shore. Suddenly, she felt something grip her upper chest tightly. The lake monster pulled her back toward it, sending up a plume of water. Katie screamed and twisted, fighting against the grasp of the creature. She heard a splash from the shore and turned to see the white spray of water, and no warrior.

Alex! Katie thought angrily. *Why didn't you stay on the shore?*

The lake monster raised part of its gray-green chest up out of the water and pulled Katie up toward its eyes and gaping mouth. The archer blinked to clear splashes from her eyes and squinted. Metal glinted around the lake monster's neck. It was a gold chain, and on the chain hung a gold key.

The archer reached for the small knife in her belt and gripped it in her hand. As the creature drew her nearer to its open jaws, she lifted the shiny chain and severed it. The links slid from the monster's neck. Katie quickly snatched the gold chain before it fell into the lake.

She had gotten a key, but now needed to escape from the creature. The archer clenched her teeth and jammed her knife into the tough skin of the monster's webbed claw. The creature howled in pain and released Katie. She fell from its grip toward the freezing water and held her breath as she plunged in, feet first. Once submerged in the cold water, she quickly kicked back up to the surface, away from the monster.

Katie saw the warrior's head pop up ahead of her. He had turned and now swam back to the shore. Between her own strokes, the archer saw Alex stumble and splash up onto the beach. She released a small sigh of relief; at least he was safe again.

After a few more strokes, Katie reached the shore as well and pulled herself up out of the freezing water. Once she stood safely on the beach, she turned to see the large lake creature writhing and tossing in the water. Then it slowly slid back down under the clear surface of the lake.

They stood on the sand, breathing heavily. A breeze chilled Katie to her bones. She shivered, shifting from one foot to the other and grasping her shoulders with her hands. The archer stared out at the rippling waters of the lake. Would the creature surface again and try to attack them? She didn't think her little jab had hurt it very much, yet it had disappeared under the water. Maybe it sank beneath the surface because she had taken its key?

The archer grinned. Katie held out the chain. "I got the key," she said, smiling.

The warrior's blue eyes glowed with glee and a broad smile spread across his bearded face. "Where was it?"

"Around the monster's neck," Katie replied.

"Wow," Alex said and looked at the archer with admiration.

Katie quickly looked down to her left and right; however she only saw the three meters and still no options to exit or save. Her health meter showed 43 percent, food showed 0 percent and weapons 66 percent. What should they do now? And why hadn't they heard any voice? Katie felt disappointed, but also drained and shaken from her experience with the monster. For the moment, Katie only wanted to get out.

"Do you see an option to exit?" Katie asked the warrior.

Alex looked down to his right and left and then shook his large head.

"How do we get out of here?" Katie sighed.

"I don't know. We could always save and exit before when me and Ty played. What's going on?" Alex shook his head, and water dripped from his long blond locks onto his broad shoulders.

Katie wondered if the game would force them along, maybe showing them where to go, so she tried to step to her left to continue along the shoreline, but her legs would not budge. She also could not move to the right. She did not want to dive into the icy waters ahead of her so she turned her back on the lake and was able to head up away from the small lapping waves. Alex followed.

They climbed up the steep and rocky hill, and into the forest. Cold, quivering and soaked, they trudged up the slope wearily. Katie stopped briefly to catch her breath. She felt very weak now in the cool shade of the trees, and her health meter only showed 38 percent. She knew they needed to either find some elixir or food, or preferably the exit.

Ahead of them, something bright caught Katie's eye. The archer frowned and squinted trying to clearly see what it was. She stepped away from the brute, leaving him behind her, breathing heavily. She jogged closer. An almost invisible, thin white line split the trees and bushes ahead. As she stepped nearer and walked to the left, she saw that the white line formed a frame around a dark center. If she had not stepped to the left, she would never have seen it. Katie excitedly turned back to Alex.

"It's a frame!" she called to the warrior.

Katie raced toward the glowing white rectangle. Heavy footfalls behind her told her that Alex ran too.

She leapt through the frame and found herself warm, dry and in a dark room. Ahead of her floated yellow words saying, "Level Achieved." Relief flowed through her. She had escaped before her health level had dropped to nothing. Then with disappointment heavy in her mind, Katie turned toward the blocky shape of Alex.

"We didn't hear a voice," Katie sighed heavily.

Alex shook his angular head slowly.

Katie removed the mask and gloves and found that Alex had done the same and they now stood in the middle of her room.

"I know this sounds crazy, but do you think it could be Ty?" Katie asked carefully, her voice barely a murmur.

"What about Ty?" Jessie whispered. Katie jumped with a start and she and Alex twisted around toward Katie's bedroom door.

"How did you get here?" Katie stammered, embarrassed that Jessie had heard what she had said.

Jessie stepped fully into Katie's bedroom and closed the door behind her stealthily. "Your mom let me in. I was worried about you after school and I tried calling and ringing the doorbell and knocking but I guess you didn't hear me. I waited until your mom got home and then asked if I could talk with you." Jessie stopped. She looked like she wanted to say more. She smoothed her wavy brown hair back. "What were you saying about Ty?"

There was no getting around it now, but Katie hesitated and then said, "This is going to sound a little crazy." Katie grasped the mask and gloves in her hands and motioned to the TV screen behind her. "We think we hear Ty in the game."

Jessie thought a moment and then spoke with worry and concern creasing her face. "You think you can hear him in a VR game?"

"I heard a voice say my name. How would a game know my name? Look, I know this sounds weird, but it did happen," Katie explained emphatically.

"I heard it say my name, too," Alex added, nodding quickly.

Jessie turned her head to the side warily. "You didn't look like you were doing anything. You were just kind of standing there frozen like zombies or something," Jessie said quietly.

"How long were you watching us?" Alex asked.

"A few minutes," Jessie replied, her frown deepening.

"We were hiking up the side of the mountain at that point," Katie said, turning to Alex. Then she asked Jessie, "It looked like we weren't moving?"

Jessie shook her head. "No, you were just standing there. I was just about ready to go get your mom, when you started moving and talking."

From the kitchen below, Audry called, "Katie, Alex, dinner is ready!"

Katie jumped and looked pleadingly at both Jessie and Alex. "Don't say a word about this."

Alex nodded quickly, but Jessie simply remained quiet.

Audry yelled up the stairs, "Jessie? Do you want to join us? I can give your mom a call."

Jessie turned to Katie and her eyes said she wanted to stay. Jessie looked at the mask and gloves Katie held in her hand. She hesitated, as if she wasn't sure about what she was going to say. Her face formed a question and her lips opened slightly, but no words came out.

Katie guessed what Jessie wanted to ask. "If you stay for dinner, we can all go back into the game."

Jessie's eyes lit up the way they used to when Ty walked into a room.

7

Katie, Jessie and Alex gulped down dinner and excused themselves from the table, quickly retreating upstairs. Alex ducked into his room and grabbed a third set of gloves and a mask. Then they all entered Katie's room and she closed the door behind them.

They stood in Katie's bedroom and, without hesitation, all three put on the gloves and masks. They found themselves standing in the dark room with powerful music surrounding them. Alex selected "Multiple Players" with his blocky, fake arm and then touched the "Choose Players" option.

Katie chose Aknia the archer woman, and Alex selected Oxtis, the warrior. Jessie studied the options and finally decided on a character called "Driana." Driana looked like she was about twenty years old and had long blonde hair pulled back into a single braid and draped over her left shoulder. She had a light face, with high cheekbones and a small, upturned nose. Beneath her small nose were pink lips and a slightly pointed chin. Her ears were topped with a gentle curve that formed a high tip. Katie smiled when she realized that Driana was an elf. What a perfect character for her friend to chose! Jessie was so like an elf, petite, usually light on her feet, happy and full of energy.

Driana wore a dark-green tunic made of a silky material. Black tights covered her legs, and on her feet she wore black cloth shoes with pointed toes. Driana floated in the area in front of Jessie.

When the weapons popped into view, Katie tried to grasp a

magic book of spells, thinking it would help them a great deal more than knives and ropes, but the frame would not light up when she pointed to the book.

"I think you can only choose it if you're a magical character," Alex said in his unreal, monotone voice, and then stated, "Driana is magical."

Jessie took the cue and reached up, touching the frame around the book, and it appeared in Driana's hands. "My display says I now have three spells, 'Fire,' 'Ice,' and 'Water,' and all I need to do is say the word to cast the spell," Jessie said, her voice sounding tin-like.

"What else is magical?" Katie's computer-generated voice asked as she scanned the choices. She found a bag of magic dust and nodded to her friend.

Jessie chose the bag and it appeared at the elf's waist, tucked up under her belt. "My display says I can use the magic dust for just about anything, except healing myself," Jessie explained as she read.

"What weapon does she come with?" Katie asked Alex.

"She has 15 fireballs. I only get 100 swings with my sword and you only get 20 arrows, unless we recharge with elixir," Alex informed his sister.

"Can we pick up weapons along the way?" Katie asked.

"Nope, you can only pick up elixir and food," Alex explained.

Katie studied the weapons again. Other items shown included a silver-tipped wooden spear. She could not imagine trying to run through a forest with that. Another frame displayed a slingshot, and another a compass. Katie shook her head to herself; she decided to stick with the knife and grappling hook. The small blade appeared in its sheath at the archer's waist and the rope and grappling hook materialized, looped through Aknia's belt. The weapons display, in yellow letters to Katie's lower right, showed 100 percent.

"We didn't save our last game, Alex. Which world should we

choose?" Katie wondered aloud in her metallic voice as the frames appeared.

"Which one were you in when you heard the voice?" Jessie asked.

"I was in the forest world," Katie said.

"Let's try the forest world," Alex said and touched the frame.

With all the weapons they had chosen, Katie thought they should be able to get through the woods and over the bog without a problem.

The music surged louder in their ears, and the frames displaying Oxtis, Driana and Aknia folded in around Alex, Jessie and Katie. Katie felt the familiar floaty, dizzying feeling as the game deposited them on the hilltop. Katie's spine tingled and she heard Jessie expel a long breath, loaded with amazement. Katie and Jessie had played other games before, but nothing like this, and Katie could hardly wait for her best friend to feel the overwhelming reality of this world.

The blue sky and grassy hilltop wrapped around them. Katie blinked as the normal light-headedness waved through her. She glanced over toward Alex and Jessie and saw the six-foot tall brute. The large warrior rocked on his heels slightly, blinked and slowly moved his head from left to right, looking at the world around him. He held the large, round shield in his left hand and the broadsword in his right as he took a cautious step forward.

Behind the warrior stood the elf. She held her arms out as if to steady herself.

"This is intense," the elf said. She raised her hand to her throat, surprised to hear the different voice escaping from her vocal chords.

Katie walked over to Jessie. "I know," the archer spoke. "It all feels so real, and it is freaky to hear another voice coming out of your mouth."

Jessie's sky-blue eyes sparkled with joy. Katie watched her friend as she placed the book of spells in a large pocket of her tunic. Then Jessie patted the black velvet bag at her waist.

"Look at your options," Alex said. "'Save' and 'Exit' don't appear again. What's going on?"

"I don't know," Katie answered. It was like the game trapped players in a level until they either ran out of health or got the key. She only wanted to avoid dangers long enough to more clearly hear the voice.

"Well," Alex said, "which way do we go?"

"This way," the archer said and lightly sidestepped down the hill-side. "I heard him in the forest."

Katie smiled to herself as they passed by a cyclone of little gnats. She reached out and swished her hand through them. The little bugs scattered, but as she continued past, she turned to watch them return to their small tornado.

The archer led the others to the bottom of the hill and leaped over the small stream. Then the three climbed the steep knoll across from the creek. Behind her, Katie heard the heavy footfalls of the warrior and the light treading of the magical elf.

"When we get into the forest," Katie explained to the other two, "there are vines that will extend out and grab you. But we should be able to get through with all the weapons we've got."

Katie hiked ahead of the others and into the woods. The air around them became cooler in the shade of the trees. As they approached the area where the vines had attacked her before, the archer crouched slightly and scanned the forest leaves and branches for movement. She knew that soon the wiry tendrils would reach out from the trees and bushes and snag them. She slowly took the small knife from the sheath at her waist and held it out in front of her.

"Watch out for the vines," Katie warned the others again. She heard rustling among the leaves and pine needles and swept the knife from side to side in front of her. Behind her, Jessie screeched.

Katie turned around and pushed Alex to the side. A vine had wrapped itself around Jessie's ankle.

The pixie screamed, "FIRE!" But to Jessie's obvious disappointment, only the vine at her ankle burst into orange flame and flashed into gray ashes. She stared in disbelief as more tendrils wriggled and stretched toward the three.

"Run!" Katie yelled.

Alex jumped out in front of the other two and pounded the earth. Katie pushed Jessie ahead of her and ran behind the pixie. More vines squirmed out of the branches and along the dirt path and grasped at their arms and legs. Alex hacked through the tendrils with his sword and cleared the way ahead of the three. Katie used her small blade to cut through any stragglers.

Suddenly, several thick vines gripped Katie's upper arms so tightly they pressed into her skin. Two more quickly slid out of the branches and gripped her wrists, restraining her. Katie cried out and Jessie stopped and looked back. Then the elf shouted to the warrior ahead. Alex turned and ran back toward Katie. Katie struggled but could not move her arms; she felt her fingers tingle as the blood was cut off.

The warrior swished his sword, easily slicing the vines. Some of the light-green fluid dripped onto Katie's bare right arm and made her itch. She scratched herself as she ran behind Alex, who once again cleared the way. Katie suddenly realized that soon they would be near the bog.

"Watch your footing," Katie called to the two ahead of her. "The ground becomes marshy and you might get sucked down into the mud."

Alex and Jessie stopped at the edge of the swamp. Katie trotted up to them and looked up over their heads. She stopped and pulled the grappling hook from her belt and started to swing it around, but as the vines encroached from behind, the archer realized there wasn't enough time for all three of them to escape. The rope wouldn't hold all of them at once, and the vines advanced too quickly for them to try to swing across one by one.

"We can climb across on the branches overhead," Katie said as she urgently pointed above. She rewound the grappling hook through her belt and leaped up, grasping the rough bark. She then swung her legs forward and back, and reached out her right arm. She continued swinging and reaching, propelling herself from one limb to another. The arrows rattled in the quiver on her back and the crossbow only slightly hindered her grip. The archer glanced over her shoulder and saw the heavy warrior struggling to find branches that would support his weight. Smaller limbs cracked and split, dropping him down toward the marsh below. The light little elf swooped along the boughs easily.

A sharp jab made Katie look up to the branch she had just attempted to grasp. A large brown thorn had nicked her finger. She pulled her hand back and quickly drew it away from the spike. She curved her other hand around the limb, her legs swinging beneath her.

"Careful!" Katie called to the others. "The branches have sharp thorns!"

Just a few more feet and they would be past the marshy area and could leap down to solid ground. Katie swung her hips again to propel herself forward. As she gripped the branch ahead of her, she lost her grip; blood had dripped from her finger down to her palm, making her hand slippery. She caught her breath and swung by her other arm over the murky waters below. She wiped the center of her hand on her pants and reached again for the branch. Katie gripped the limb and then heard Alex cry out in his low, rumbling voice.

The archer looked at the large warrior and saw a thorn sticking through his left hand. Katie winced, feeling the sharp pain with Alex. Alex lifted his hand up off the spike, groaning with pain as it tore through his palm. He grimaced and held his hand to his chest, dangling by one muscular arm.

"You okay?" Katie shouted to him, concern cracking her voice.

Alex nodded slowly, his bearded face contorted with discomfort. He struggled, but then reached up and gripped the branch above him with his bleeding hand.

"Just a little bit farther and we can drop to the ground," Katie said encouraging her brother.

Alex swung his legs again and reached for the next branch, grunting with effort. Katie kicked herself ahead and saw Jessie clear the marsh and effortlessly drop to the ground. A small cloud puffed up as the elf landed in the dirt. Katie sighed with relief; at least one of them had made it to the other side of the bog. A few more swings and Katie too had cleared the marsh. She dropped to the ground and turned and watched Alex gingerly gripping and swinging from branch to branch. Red blood had dripped from his palm down his arm. He gave his legs a final swing and thudded to the ground where he crumpled and then plopped to his knees. Katie and Jessie rushed to his side. He held his injured hand by the wrist and extended his fingers.

"It *hurts*," Alex stated, looking up at Katie with a frown, and Katie almost cried because she had never meant for her brother to be harmed. He then glanced down to his lower right. "My health is down to 95 percent."

"We need to wrap your hand up with something," Katie said as she gripped the edge of her cloth tunic and started to tear it.

"No, wait," Alex said, motioning to the elf. "The magic dust can be used to heal. Or we can look for elixir." Jessie pulled the black velvet bag open and sprinkled golden sparkles on Alex's hand. Instantly, the bleeding stopped and the hole in the palm of his hand closed up.

"My health is back up to 100 percent," Alex said, smiling as he flexed his fingers and made a fist.

Katie sighed with relief and then noticed that her own health meter displayed 98 percent. Her finger had stopped bleeding but still stung.

"Do you need some dust, too?" Jessie asked.

"No," Katie said, shaking her head. "I don't want you to use up all of your magic dust. Maybe we can find some elixir."

"There should be some around here somewhere," Alex said and with effort he pushed himself up from the ground.

They stood in a clearing bordered by small bushes. Beyond the brush grew tall pines and leafy trees.

"Let's see if we can find some elixir," Katie suggested. She could drink a little, just enough to heal her finger, and then they could save the rest.

The three separated, each taking a different area, and swished through the thick green leaves, searching for a blue bottle. Suddenly, the elf screamed a high, quick shriek. Katie snapped her head up and turned to look toward Jessie. The elf gripped her left ankle and sat heavily on the ground.

Katie shouted, "Vines!" and she raced toward Jessie.

As she and Alex ran over to Jessie, Katie saw two small drops of blood through tears in the black tights on the elf's left leg.

"Something bit me," Jessie said as she gripped her lower leg in both hands.

Katie knelt next to Jessie and examined the bloody spots. "Fangs," she gasped. "Must have been a snake!"

"Uh-oh," Jessie said and her eyes grew wide as she looked down to her lower right.

"What does your health meter say?" Alex stammered.

"It says eighty percent." Jessie's voice strained and suddenly got higher and more frightened. "It's going lower!"

"Poison," Alex said, looking at Katie. "We have to find some elixir!"

The two raced away from Jessie and continued searching for a blue bottle, taking care to watch for movement as they rustled through leaves and in bushes.

"Sixty!" Jessie called out from where she sat on the ground.

"Is there a specific place where you can find this stuff?" Katie shouted, frustrated.

"There was some in the castle so I think there should be some out here," Alex said as he swept through leaves.

"Forty!" Jessie cried. Katie glanced back and saw her friend's face grow pale. Jessie moaned, "I feel sick."

"Hold on!" Katie cried. If they didn't find elixir and the elf's health ran out, what would happen then?

"Found it!" Alex yelled and raised a glowing blue bottle up over his head. Katie and Alex raced back to Jessie's side. Alex handed the pixie the container and she drank two quick gulps and took a breath. She drank another two swallows and stared to her right, breathing deeply.

"Sixty," She sighed and then raised the bottle to her lips and sipped more of the fluid.

Alex placed his hand on Jessie's shoulder and gently said, "Leave some for Katie."

"I will," the pixie said, nodding. She took four more gulps of the glowing liquid and handed the bottle to Katie.

Katie put the container to her lips and let the remaining fluid flow into her mouth. It was sweet and cold and tasted good. Katie glanced over to her health meter and saw that it had risen back up to 100 percent.

Thank goodness they had made it this far, but Katie felt disappointed: they had not heard any voice. Katie stood with her hands on her hips, the crossbow pressing slightly into her left side. *Where do we go from here?*

The massive warrior stepped up next to the archer and asked, "What now?"

"I don't know." Katie shook her head and ran her right hand through her short brown hair. She looked down in front of her and did not see options to save or exit. A trail led off through the brush and into the denser forest. Should they take the path? They still had Alex's sword, two of Jessie's spells and a lot of magic dust, let alone the archer's knife, crossbow and grappling hook with rope. "Let's take the trail," Katie said and she glanced over to her two companions.

They trudged up the dusty pathway a few hundred feet and soon Katie saw a frame hovering in the air. She raced for the white rectangle and the three hopped through it and into the dark room. Ahead of her in yellow letters were the words, "Level Failed." Then the screen changed and "Single Player" and "Multiple Players" were displayed again.

"Do we have time to play again?" Alex asked.

Katie instinctively raised her left hand but instead of seeing her watch on her wrist, she saw her blocky arm. "It can't be more than six-thirty or seven," Katie said and she looked to the rectangular shapes to her left. "Should we?"

Jessie shrugged her squared shoulders and Alex nodded his blocky head. Why not?

8

Katie chose the "Multiple Players" option and waited for the next selection to appear. After picking the same characters and weapons, Katie wanted to see if she could start the game where they had left off — in the bushes and trees — but Alex reached up and selected the castle world before Katie could do anything about it.

Immediately the gray stone walls of the castle swam in around the three players. Goosebumps formed on Katie's skin and she shivered as the cold air of the citadel enveloped her. She glanced over at Alex. He stood stiff as a board, almost afraid to breathe. Then he stepped forward and watched his feet touch the stone floor.

Jessie clutched her upper arms and whispered, "It's cold in here."

Katie nodded to her friend in agreement. It was very chilly but more than that, Katie didn't like the way the stone walls made her feel. They gave her the uncomfortable sense of being closed in — trapped. "Which way do we go?" the archer wondered aloud.

"I've played the castle level before," Alex said. "I'll lead the way." The warrior pulled the broadsword from the sheath at his waist and stepped ahead of the other two down the passageway.

Katie loaded an arrow in her crossbow and Jessie walked quietly to Katie's right. Katie concentrated with all her being. *Ty, if it is really you, answer me. Let me know you are here.* Only silence responded. She heard no voice, felt no presence.

At the first turn, the warrior led the three to the right. They continued down the corridor and, at the next junction, turned to the left.

As Katie stepped out around Alex and jogged up the hallway, the shuffle of her feet echoed through the corridor. She quickly retrieved a bag and her food display then showed 100 percent.

Alex and Jessie trotted up behind Katie. The archer broke off a piece of cheese and handed one chunk to the brute and one to the elf. "Taste it," she said, smiling with anticipation.

The elf and warrior placed the morsels in their mouths. Alex rolled his eyes as he chewed. He swallowed and shook his head with disbelief. The elf raised her eyebrows as she chewed.

"Amazing isn't it?" Katie asked, and Alex and Jessie nodded in agreement.

Katie sighed and pointed down the corridor. "If we go this way and turn to the right, we'll be trapped by moving walls." Alex knowingly nodded and Katie thought he must have also been trapped in a previous game. "Let's go to the left," Katie said.

Katie led the three to the left and up the new hallway. At the end of the passageway, another juncture opened into corridors on both the left and right.

Katie stood in the archway, debating which way to go, when she suddenly felt a strange eeriness that made her skin crawl. She knew Alex and Jessie stood behind her, and she was aware of their presence, but something else was there, too – a heavy, yet almost imperceptible presence. She quickly turned around and asked, "Do you feel that?"

Jessie lowered her head and moved her eyes from side to side, but then she shook her head. Alex, breathing shallowly, also shook his head with disappointment. "But *you* feel something, don't you, Katie?" Alex asked.

Katie nodded and started to speak, but Alex gripped her arm and hushed her to silence. "There are soldiers in the castle," he said urgently.

Could it be one of them Katie sensed? She extended her left arm out, and slowly leveled the crossbow toward the corridor behind them, watching for any motion. Then, out of the corner of her eye, she thought she saw a shadow creep across the wall to her left and thought she felt something brush up against her shoulder. Katie stood perfectly still and gazed at the stone, eyes wide, breath quick, all of her senses heightened. She only heard the sputter of the torch's flame. The hairs on the back of her neck prickled and a string of tickles ran down her spine. She saw no movement, heard no sound except the torch's flutter, the flow of her own breathing and the pulsing of her heart in her ears.

Then it was gone.

Katie swallowed a dry gulp. The prickles on the back of her neck died down, but her heart still pounded.

"Did you feel anything? Did you see anything?" Katie turned desperately to her two companions. Jessie and Alex both shook their heads.

"What was it?" Jessie murmured into Katie's ear.

"It's something scary. A presence. Hard to explain," Katie whispered, still shaken.

"There might be other things in the castle that we don't know about," Alex reminded Katie warily.

Katie knew her brother was right. There could be all kinds of creepy creatures lurking around in these dark corridors. "Let's go," Katie said shakily as she cautiously pushed past the large warrior and the small elf and continued down the left corridor. She wanted to put distance between herself and the strange, eerie hallway.

At the end of the passageway, another juncture appeared with an opening to the left and one to the right. The hallway to the left ended with a large wooden door.

What could be behind the door? Katie wondered. A key? A monster? Ty?

Katie knew they must search for the key to this level, so she led the others forward. When she grabbed the heavy latch carefully with her right hand and pressed her thumb down, the wood released slightly from the doorjamb. Before opening it farther, Katie swept her left arm behind her in a signal for the others to stay back. The archer slowly swung the heavy door inward, her crossbow loaded and ready. The door slid open freely and Katie swept the completely dark room with her gaze before stepping forward.

Katie kept her eyes on the chamber and watched for any shadow or motion. She whispered over her shoulder, "Alex, grab a torch and hand it to me, okay?"

Alex slipped a few feet back down the hallway, pulled a torch out of its bracket on the wall and carried it back to the archer. "Here," Alex said as he held the handle out for Katie. The archer woman reached back across herself, and grasped it quickly with her right hand. She held the torch up in front of her and stepped cautiously into the room.

The small chamber was empty. As Katie slowly moved the light, it illuminated the crevasses of the gray brick walls. She then saw something sparkling in the cracks. As the light from the flame passed over the bricks, the sparkles began to drip and formed pools of bright blue that glistened in the torchlight. Katie watched with disbelief as the pools formed small, blue, spidery creatures. Suddenly they skittered across the floor and began to bite Katie, Alex and Jessie's feet and ankles. As the sharp teeth pierced Katie's skin, she cried out, jumping back away and kicking, trying to knock the things off her feet. Alex yelled, Jessie shouted, and they both shook their feet, trying to knock the creatures loose.

Katie swept the torch downward and the things screeched and skittered away. The first group of spidery creatures backed off, retreating into the chamber, but more and more formed from the dripping blue fluid and advanced slowly toward Katie, Jessie and

Alex. Katie reached for the handle and, holding the torch between herself and the creatures, she pulled the door closed.

Katie dropped the torch at the bottom of the door, turned quickly, grabbed Alex and Jessie by the arms and ran back down the hallway, leaving the screeching, scratching creatures behind them, closed in the small, dark room.

What a mistake! She needed to be more careful. They hurried down the passageway. When Katie felt they had put enough distance between themselves and the spidery things, they stopped running.

"Weird," Alex breathed. He bent at the waist, hands on his hips, trying to catch his breath.

Katie nodded, panting. She looked at the warrior's feet and pointed. "Blood," she said. Then she looked at the elf's feet. Jessie had been bitten as well, although not as severely. Katie's own feet stung with the painful bites. She glanced to her right and noticed that her health meter read 90 percent.

Jessie sprinkled some golden magic dust on Katie and Alex's feet. Warm tingling spread through Katie's bites and in a few seconds the pulsating pain stopped.

"Thanks. We need to find elixir for you," Katie said, nodding to the elf. "What does your health meter show?"

"Ninety-three percent," Jessie replied, not worried.

Katie felt she should be all right until they found elixir – or a key. Katie continued their exploration by leading the way down the castle corridor. As she approached the end of the hallway, she saw more light. It glowed bright yellow like sunlight instead of the faint flame of torches. They continued down the passageway and Katie saw an open door leading to the illuminated room. Before entering the chamber, Katie glanced from right to left, looking at either side of the doorway. There did not seem to be anything or anyone near. She entered the room and quickly spun around to scan the area behind them. Cautiously, Alex and Jessie stepped in as well. No one else stood in the room except for the archer, pixie and warrior. Alex extended his thumb up.

In the center of the chamber sat a high-backed throne covered in dark red velvet. The chair was very ornate; gold tassels dangled from the corners and gold buttons adorned the upholstery.

Katie looked up to the high ceiling, then her gaze flowed to the three long, narrow windows cut into the wall opposite the throne. Thick, dark-red velvet drapes hung on either side of the openings and dusted the floor. The windows laid out strips of bright yellow sunlight on the gray stone floor of the castle.

Katie stepped across the room to examine the fancy chair and passed through a stream of sunlight. Warmth coated her cool skin as she walked into the sunbeam and she paused. She blinked, squinted and looked out the window. The archer felt heat on her upturned face. Then she walked out of the light stream.

To her left, as she stood facing the throne, Katie saw the doorway through which they had entered. The large, wooden door, with metal hinges shaped like sculpted triangles, stood open. Behind the ornate chair was another wooden door and to her right was another; both were closed. As the three stood examining the area, Katie heard voices and loud tromping coming from the right. Katie looked at Jessie, who stood next to the throne, petting the thick upholstery. Jessie looked up with fright. Katie then glanced at Alex, who stood in the sunbeam, mouth open, turning his arms slowly in the warmth of the light.

"Hide!" Katie whispered urgently.

The archer quickly stepped over to the heavy drapes on either side of the long, narrow windows. She saw the warrior and the elf sweep behind the velvet as well. The thick material would hide them, and the velvet dropped to the ground so their feet would not be visible.

"Yes, sire," a voice announced as the large, wooden door slowly creaked open. "The guards have traced their presence to this area."

Katie quietly sucked in a breath. The soldiers knew they were near! Hopefully the guards wouldn't search the room. She relaxed a bit, knowing that the tight weave of the drapes hid her. Just below her right eye, a small tear in the fabric allowed her to see through the material. She saw a man, presumably the one who had spoken, holding the door open. He wore metal armor over his chest and carried a sword in a shiny sheath at his side.

A man dressed like a king sauntered into the room. A gold crown sat atop his brown hair and he wore a long, green velvet robe. He walked grandly up to the throne and sat down. The armored man, apparently a captain, shouted an order out toward the hallway. A troop of eight soldiers marched into the chamber; their metal armor clanked and creaked.

Another man stepped silently into the room and stood apart from the soldiers, the captain and the king. This man had thick, graying black hair and a black beard salted with gray. He scanned the room intently with his dark eyes. He wore a dark-brown leather tunic and trousers made of the same; black gloves covered his hands.

The soldiers formed a line in front of the throne, with their armored backs to the long windows and drapes. Katie heard a soldier's heavy breathing. She watched in amazement as a drop of sweat slid down one soldier's brow to the thick brown beard that covered his cheeks. The soldiers all smelled of pungent perspiration, and Katie almost gagged from the stench.

The captain of the soldiers spoke to the king: "The first division has surrounded the castle. No one can escape."

The king stroked his dark-brown beard as he listened. When the captain had finished speaking, the king pronounced, "Good, good. We shall have them by nightfall." He petted his beard again. "The prisoners shall not escape and they shall pay for their crimes," the king announced.

What had the characters done in this game? Katie wondered. *Why did the soldiers want to capture them?*

"Grevnon, have the traps all been put into place?" the king asked.

The gray-haired man hissed, "Yes, my Lord Ristis." His voice had fullness to it unlike the other characters, and when Katie noticed this, it frightened her.

The king, captain and soldiers all seemed programmed. They talked as if they recited lines in a play, but the gray-haired man was different. He spoke with emotion and his actions mystified Katie as she watched him carefully through the tear in the fabric. The others seemed stiff and automatic, but he moved fluidly and stealthily, seeming to ignore his fellow characters and almost acting as if he were not part of the game. He skulked around the room, as if he were searching for Katie, Jessie and Alex. No, she realized with sudden panic and disbelief, he was not looking for them, but *feeling* for them. It was as if he sensed that they were there. Katie became increasingly fearful of him. She did not understand why he acted the way he did, but she did know that it terrified her. Katie withdrew inwardly, trying to mask her presence.

"I'm here, Katie. Can you see me?" Like a breath, the voice spoke.

Katie almost cried out. The voice called her by name again! Whoever it was must be near, or else why would he ask if she could see him? Katie held her tongue because of the gray-haired man, Grevnon. She felt scared and did not want him to discover where they hid.

The king waved his hand in a manner to signal that the eight soldiers should go about their business. The clanking guards, and their captain, filed out, leaving the king and the gray-haired man. As the soldiers marched by, their stench wafted past Katie. She held her breath.

"Let us go to the dining hall. It is almost time to sup," the king said as he rose from his throne and strode out of the room. Grevnon followed, but at the doorway he paused. He slowly turned back and gazed over the interior. Katie tried to calm her heavily beating heart. Could he see her through the tear? She feared that the thundering in her chest would give her away. She did not want to be found by this man. He was beyond creepy. She thought he acted and seemed more real than anything else in the game. He made Katie's virtual skin crawl.

Katie's heart beat faster and her body became rigid. It seemed that minutes passed. Finally, Grevnon's mouth curled up in a slow, sly smile, then he turned and left the room.

Why did he smile? Did he know they were there? If he did, why didn't he march over, yank the drapes from in front of them and call the guards? Instead he acted as if he knew they were there but let them be. Why?

After a few seconds, Katie began to breathe again. She stepped cautiously from behind the heavy velvet. Alex and Jessie emerged slowly from the drapes behind which they had hidden and Katie turned toward them. "Did you see that man?" she whispered.

"What man?" Jessie replied quietly. "I couldn't see anything."

"I couldn't either," Alex said in a low voice.

"But I heard the voice," Jessie affirmed quietly. Katie stared at the elf with wide eyes. "I heard it say your name and ask if you could see him."

Alex nodded. "I heard it, too."

They had heard it, too. Katie wasn't sure if that made her feel happy or sad. Did that mean they were all going crazy?

"I don't understand why he doesn't just show himself," Katie said as she scanned the room.

"Maybe he's not in here," Jessie said with a little shiver in her voice as she warily looked around.

Maybe he is outside, Katie thought. They had entered from the left and the soldiers and others had exited through the door to the right. Maybe he was through the door straight ahead?

Katie stepped forward to the door behind the throne. Caution told her to be ready: There could be soldiers outside. She held her crossbow out in front of her and heard the soft swipe of the sword as Alex unsheathed his weapon. Katie looked back behind her to make sure Jessie followed, and the elf nodded assuringly to her. Then Katie pushed the heavy door open with effort. She felt her heart beat faster and faster with anticipation as she walked into the cool passageway.

She saw an archway ahead of them and approached it cautiously. Under her feet, she felt the floor change from cold stone to hollow wood. She had already taken a few steps onto the planks, concentrating more on the archway ahead of her than the flooring, when she realized that she stood on a trap door. She stopped and Alex and Jessie bumped into her. Katie looked down just as the boards fell away beneath them.

Gravity pulled at her stomach as she tumbled down, down into darkness. She heard Alex yell and Jessie scream, and felt the rattle of a shriek in her own throat. In a few seconds, she felt a crushing pain jolt through her body as she impacted with the floor.

Their surroundings went completely dark and two large yellow words displayed, "Game Over."

Katie slowly removed the mask from her eyes and blinked, light-headed and disoriented. She glanced over to where Alex stood. He removed his mask and massaged his temples. Jessie dropped the gloves and mask to the floor. She trembled, breathed heavily and stared wide-eyed down at the objects.

Katie felt a warm liquid slide out of her right nostril. Her right hand shot up to her nose. She swiped the fluid and held her finger out to see – blood!

Katie stepped over by her bed, grabbed a tissue and held it tightly up against her nose. She couldn't believe it. Had the fall made her nose bleed, or would it have bled just the same if she had not played the game? Katie felt suddenly very guilty. Jessie had crumpled to the floor and looked pale and ill. Alex stood stiff, holding the mask in his hands and staring at it with disbelief.

"I'm sorry," Katie said, dabbing the blood from her nose. With relief she realized it had already quit bleeding.

Jessie looked up to Katie and frowned. "Sorry for what?" she asked.

"I'm sorry I talked you into this. It made me feel sick a couple of times and I should have warned you about it. Oh, this is impossible!" Katie moaned. "What was I thinking?" Katie sat heavily on the edge of her bed.

Jessie stood up and walked over to Katie. Then she sat next to her friend and placed her arm around Katie's shoulder. "Don't be sorry. It's okay. We'll just have to try again. Maybe tomorrow." Katie looked into Jessie's green-brown eyes and instantly became calm. "I don't understand this either, but I heard it. I know I did," Jessie said.

Alex stepped closer and nodded. "We have to try again, tomorrow, after school."

Katie nodded. Jessie said it was getting late and that she should head home. She hugged Katie, told her not to worry and to get some rest. Then she lightly stepped from Katie's room.

Alex left too and soon Katie heard the water running in the shower. Katie leaned over onto her side. She would wait until Alex was done and then get ready for bed. But how could she possibly sleep?

9

The next day, Katie rushed from class to class with more anxiety and anticipation than on any other Friday. She ached for the hours to pass quickly. She could not walk through the hallways without her imagination drowning out the echoes of the students' voices and replacing them with the silent whispers of leather boots on stone floors. She could not sit in class surrounded by classmates without feeling alone and trapped by strangling vines. She could not step down the gray concrete sidewalk without seeing the trees on the school grounds become thick forests.

At lunch, with great effort, Katie and Jessie talked about everything *except* the game. The others at the table giggled and speculated about which boy liked which girl. Katie and Jessie played along, laughing nervously and agreeing that Justin must find Alyson pretty. Jessie nervously glanced at Katie; her eyes silently wished that the day would end, and Katie agreed with a smile.

Katie struggled through her afternoon classes and finally, after the last electronic bell signaled the end of the day, she sped through the halls, forgetting her math book and homework, focusing only on getting to Jessie's car.

Katie stood waiting by the vehicle and saw Jessie run through the parking lot. When Jessie reached the car, she quickly unlocked the car doors and both girls piled in. Neither of them spoke as Jessie drove directly to Katie's house.

Katie unlocked the front door, and, after they both slid inside, she slammed it shut and raced up to her room with Jessie right behind her. Katie powered on the game system and TV. The screen flickered to life. Jessie and Katie tugged the gloves onto their hands and waited impatiently for Alex to get home.

Finally the front door thudded open, then shut, and Alex pounded up the stairs and burst into Katie's room.

"Ready?" he asked breathlessly.

"Yep," Katie replied and handed him his gloves and mask.

With all of their fingers and faces covered, the game displayed the familiar prompts. Katie again chose the brown-haired archer. The figure of Aknia floated just in front of Katie. For her weapons, she again selected the small blade, rope and grappling hook. Jessie pointed to the braided elf, book of spells and magic dust. Alex picked the blond warrior. But, at Katie's urging, they slowly looked through the brute's possible weapons.

A bow and quiver of arrows was displayed, but Alex's figure curled his blocky lip. "I just want the helmet and shield," Alex said. The young teen's shape reached up and touched the frames for the two items and they materialized on the warrior's image.

When the game displayed the "Choose World" prompt, Katie hesitated. Which world should they choose? Katie selected the castle world because it was where they had last heard the voice. The stone walls and corridors of the castle drew in around them. Torches nearest them fluttered, as if their arrival had disturbed the flame.

Katie fought the normal dizziness and looked around. Unlike the corridor they had appeared in previously, which split off to the right, this hallway extended straight and had no junctions. Had they started the game in a different spot? The archer noticed that the stone floor sloped slightly downward from where they stood. Where would it take them? *Only one way to find out,* Katie thought and led the way, following the slanting surface.

The passageway became wider as they walked along. Ahead of

her, the corridor disappeared into empty blackness. Katie grabbed a torch, preparing to light their way once they crossed into the darkness. She paused and extended her left hand out to touch the stone archway between the corridor and the darkness beyond. She held the torch out in front, but looked back toward Alex and Jessie, making sure they stayed close. As they stepped up behind her, Katie again turned forward and walked into the cavern.

The darkness of the huge cave ate up the light from the torch. Katie craned her neck back and saw the light from the flames lick into the rocky crags of the high ceiling above. She looked to the sides but could barely see the detail of the wide, rough walls around them. Katie, followed by Alex and Jessie, cautiously stepped down the path through the cavern.

Katie felt a strange tingle up her spine, as if something watched them. She scanned the shadows cast across the rocks for movement as she continued forward. They had only advanced a short way when Katie heard rustling, and shuffling coming from the dark to their left. A low growl vibrated through the ground. The archer felt the earth shudder as something large plodded out of the darkness.

Katie turned back to the warrior and elf. The three looked at each other wide-eyed. What could it be? Katie did not want to stick around to find out. The archer motioned for the others to go ahead of her, then sprang into a run. As she sprinted, the ground beneath her shook with tremors from the plodding footfalls of a giant creature.

Katie rushed as fast as she could down the pathway. The cave darkness surrounded her and the others, except for the small glow of light that bounded across the path and rocky walls from the torch she carried as she ran. Alex and Jessie staggered to a halt a few steps ahead of Katie. Katie caught up, and the illumination from the torch revealed a rock wall directly in front of them. The thundering footsteps behind them sent a jolt of adrenaline through Katie.

Katie lifted the torch, illuminating the gray granite to her left and right; she darted about, trying to find an escape route. She raised her head and saw a gouge of darkness above them, cut into the rock wall. It looked like the opening to a tunnel. It seemed to be their only chance.

"Up!" Katie shouted and pointed. She held the light high, attempting to reveal the opening several feet over their heads. Katie then handed the torch to Alex; he held it in his right hand and gripped his shield in his left. The archer quickly removed the rope and grappling hook from her belt. As she swung the rope over her head, the others cleared away. She tossed the rope up into the higher cave opening, but it arced past the gap and fell back to the ground.

Behind them the creature plodded closer. The ground shook with its footfalls and yellow flames licked nearer and nearer the three. *What could it be?* Katie's mind raced. *A fire-breathing dragon?*

"Hurry!" Alex prodded Katie.

An ear-warping roar erupted behind them. Katie, Alex and Jessie spun around to face the creature. It *was* a dragon. It reared its spiny head and flashed its black, forked tongue. The dragon studied the three figures with its red, fiery eyes. Around its greenish-black, scaly neck, a golden chain twinkled, and on the chain swung a golden key.

Impossible! Katie thought. They'd have to get closer to the dragon's sharp teeth and flaming breath before they'd be able to grasp the key!

Jessie held the small black book in front of her and shouted, "ICE!" toward the dragon, just as it expelled a huge tongue of fire. The yellow, red and orange flares froze in mid-air as they exited the dragon's jaws, then crashed to the floor, sending thousands of shattered, frozen flames skittering across the stone.

Katie looked at her crossbow and almost instantly realized that the small shafts would not deter the huge dragon. She shot an arrow anyway. It bounced off the dragon's chest, since it could not penetrate the thick scales.

Jessie stuffed the book back into her pocket, then linked her thumbs together, held her arms out and cupped her hands. Within her palms a small yellow glow formed and grew brighter and larger. Heat and energy radiated from Jessie's curved fingers. The elf opened up her hands and released a fireball toward the dragon. The flaming ball smashed against the creature's spiny skull with a sizzle. The beast howled and raised its gigantic head upward toward the rocky ceiling of the cave.

Its pained and angry howl sent a shiver up Katie's spine. Fireballs would hold the dragon off for a while, but she needed to act quickly to help them escape. She shakily swung the rope and grappling hook again, and this time the hook snagged in the rocks above them. Katie tugged on the rope and it held.

"Go up!" she shouted to the warrior and elf.

"You go first," Jessie called over her shoulder, thumbs linked together. "I can shoot fireballs at him to keep him away." Jessie aimed her palms toward the beast and released another ball of flame.

"I think I'm too heavy," Alex said as he held out his arms and looked down his huge body.

Katie breathed quickly and glanced from the rope to Alex and Jessie. Should she leave the others behind? As another fireball flew toward the dragon, Katie thought that Jessie could definitely hold off the creature. *I'll climb up and hold the rope in place so Alex can get away. Then Jessie shouldn't have any trouble.*

The archer grabbed the rope and pulled herself up, hand over hand. She pressed her legs against the rock wall, walking up the cracks and crags as she climbed. She heard the sizzle of another fireball and the roar of the dragon's flame and saw illumination from behind her. Jessie still held the beast at bay.

Katie's arms began to ache and tremble. The crossbow on her left arm twisted, but its straps held it in place. Just a few more feet and finally the upper ledge drew closer. Katie scraped her knuckles against the lip of the cave as she reached the top, swung her leg up and scrambled over the rocky edge. She quickly turned and grasped the rope.

"C'mon!" Katie urgently called back down.

Jessie let another fireball fly toward the dragon. Katie watched the flaming orb impact on the dragon's side. The creature's head snapped around and it licked at its wound.

Alex dropped the torch and his shield, grasped the rope, and started up. Katie held the upper end of the rope to make sure it didn't slip. The twine pulled taut in her hands and creaked under the warrior's weight. The grappling hook slipped and pulled a few small rocks loose. The small rocks, dirt and gravel spilled out over the edge of the cave entrance and peppered the warrior's bearded face. Alex quickly looked down and away to keep from getting dust and dirt in his eyes.

Katie desperately grasped the end of the rope and tried to keep the hook from coming loose, but Alex was too heavy. The iron broke free of the rocks. Alex fell to the cave floor with a thud. The rope spun into a pile around him and the hook clattered against the ground.

Katie watched Jessie look away from the dragon and toward the warrior. The archer almost shouted a warning, but the creature moved too fast, saw its opportunity and shot a string of flame that hit the elf's left shoulder as she sensed the creature's attack and ducked. The flare set the sleeve of Jessie's garment on fire, and she cried out and grasped her shoulder, quickly snuffing out the flame with the palm of her right hand. Alex jumped to his feet as another flare shot toward Jessie's turned head. Facing the elf, Alex leapt into the path of the fire, and it scorched his back. Katie watched helplessly as Alex arched his spine and tumbled to the cave floor, screaming from the burning pain.

Katie wailed in horror, wide-eyed, staring below her. The sick smell of burned flesh floated up to her. Alex writhed weakly on the cave floor. Jessie blinked, steadied herself and then shot a quick fireball at the dragon to keep it away for a few more seconds. The dragon roared and growled as the fireball hit it squarely between the eyes.

Alex lay motionless a few feet away from Jessie. The dragon snapped at Alex's right ankle, trying to grasp the warrior and drag him away. The torch, now lying on the cave floor, sputtered and sent weird shadows across the rocky walls.

Desperate to keep the creature away from her brother and her friend, Katie shot another arrow at the dragon. It stuck between scales, but the dragon did not react. It had no effect! She had nothing she could use to help the elf and warrior trapped below.

Katie surveyed the scene in horror. Was Alex unconscious? Would he survive? The burn looked terrible! His tunic back gaped open, exposing blackened skin beneath. Katie knew that Jessie's shoulder throbbed with pain also, yet Jessie still faced the relentless, huge dragon. Katie quickly looked down to the left and right, but knew immediately that she would not see the options to save or exit. They had to play out the scene! She looked to the cave below her. What could she do to help the others? Nothing! And the torch's flame would soon sputter out!

Jessie formed and shot another bright-yellow fireball across the cave, just as the torch snuffed out. The flaming ball exploded on the dragon's head. Katie saw the creature rear up again in agony. As soon as the fireball's light faded, darkness consumed the cave.

Unable to see anything, Katie slipped back from the edge. She extended her right palm out, feeling for the rough rock, looked toward her hand but could see nothing. Her fingers touched the granite wall and she steadied herself. Now what? The archer searched the blackness below, desperate for any light. She felt the dragon's growl vibrate through the ground and walls, and the sound sent a terrible chill up her spine. Could it see in the dark? Would it continue to attack Jessie and Alex?

Suddenly a fireball illuminated the cave. Katie saw the motion-less warrior and stalking dragon. She watched as the flaming orb missed the creature, and impacted on the rocky wall. Before the light from the fireball faded, Jessie reached forward, grabbed onto Alex's left arm, and pulled him toward her.

The cavern fell into complete and utter darkness once again. Katie listened intently for any sound to determine what could be happening below. Why had she scrambled up the rope and left them to fend for themselves? Would they have to get the key from the dragon in order to exit?

A low rumbling trembled through the cave. It did not come from below — from the dragon — but seemed to come from every-where else. The entire cavern shuddered and, as the shaking contin-ued, small rocks and sandy dust pecked at Katie's head and shoul-ders. A portion of the ceiling slowly crumbled open with the quaking rumble, allowing streams of sunlight to flow into the cavern.

Sunbeams washed over the dragon's head and back. Where the bright rays touched the dragon's scales, a hissing sizzle sounded. The creature screeched and growled. It reeled back and roared loudly, deafening Katie with its screams of pain. She covered her ears as it retreated noisily into the cold darkness of the cave. As it crept away, a hissing, misty smoke flowed off its scaly back.

Wide-eyed, Jessie looked up at Katie with her sky-blue eyes. "I threw magic dust up into the air and wished it," Jessie said, and her face glowed with amazement.

"Wished what?" Katie asked breathlessly.

"I wished for light," Jessie said, smiling.

Katie pointed urgently to the motionless brute lying on the floor. "Is he okay?"

Jessie knelt down beside the warrior and spoke softly. "Alex."

Katie relaxed a bit as she saw the large, hairy barbarian's eyelids flutter. Alex opened his eyes and grabbed the elf. Katie thought he must believe the dragon still threatened them.

Jessie patted Alex on the arm. "It's gone. The sunlight burned the dragon," she said, motioning up toward the crack in the roof of the cave. "It's gone now, back into the dark."

Alex sighed and relaxed, but tensed again. He sat up, let out a groan of pain and reached for his back.

Jessie sprinkled magic dust over Alex's scorched skin and the warrior winced. Katie cringed with him. An expression of relief soon spread across the brute's bearded face. He looked down to his left and right and then frowned. Katie realized that he too looked for the meters and she looked for them herself. No health percentage, no food meter, not even a display for weapons appeared. What was going on now?

"I can't tell if my health is back up," Alex said as he pushed himself up off the cave floor and stretched his arms and back. Katie saw only fresh pink skin through the gap in the warrior's tunic. "Maybe we have to finish the level before the menus come back?" Alex wondered, looking up toward his sister.

"I don't know," Katie said as she shook her head. Then she pursed her lips together and said, "I've got to climb back down."

"No, wait," Alex said, holding up his hands. "That's the only way out. I don't want to go back past that dragon." Alex shivered with fear, and worry creased his broad face.

"Where does that lead?" Jessie asked, pointing behind Katie.

The archer twisted to stare down the dark passageway behind her. "I don't know, I can't see," Katie said, her voice coated with uncertainty.

"I still think that's the only way out," Alex insisted.

"I think he's right, Katie," Jessie affirmed. "It looks like the only possible way."

Katie felt doubtful. She didn't know what could be in the tunnel behind her. It could be a dead end, or maybe some other creature lurked in the dark. Should she climb down and then the three of them try to sneak past the dragon? If it did attack them again, they had magic dust, but what if it injured Jessie? She could not use the dust to heal herself, and what would happen if she were injured badly?

Below her, Alex tested the cave wall, trying to find footholds and handholds, but the rocks jutting out were not large enough to allow him to climb up to where Katie stood.

Katie watched her brother struggle and realized they would need to use the rope. "Toss me the hook," Katie called down to her brother.

The warrior picked up the rope and grappling hook, swung it in a small circle, released the heavy iron and watched it sail up toward the waiting archer. Katie snagged it out of the air.

The archer shoved two of the hooks firmly between cracks in the cave wall. She nodded down to the brute. It was ready for him to try. Alex tugged on the rope, but it came loose and Katie grabbed it before it could drop down over the edge.

She tried again. She slammed the grappling hook into a crack in the cave wall, knocking pieces of the gray rock loose, but the metal claw did not remain wedged. The rope slipped from Katie's grip and slid down over the edge of the cave. The hook clanked against the stone floor as it landed.

"What do we do now?" Alex threw the rope to the ground, exasperated.

Katie stood with her hands on her hips, then dropped her arms to her sides. Her mouth hung open as she looked beyond the frustrated warrior to the elf. Jessie floated a few feet above the ground; magic dust sparkled on her black cloth shoes.

Jessie looked at Katie, shrugged her shoulders and tipped her head to the side. "I can fly."

"I see that," Katie said. "Uh, see if you can fly with Alex holding on." Katie pointed toward the large warrior.

Jessie floated closer to the ground and held her arms out for the brute. Alex snagged the rope and hook from the ground, then awkwardly looped one arm around the elf's waist as he placed one foot on top of her left shoe. Jessie groaned with effort and swallowed hard and grimaced as she attempted to balance herself and the bulky warrior above the ground.

"He's heavy," she said, wincing. The elf pinched her small, delicate features into harsh wrinkles. She squeezed her eyelids shut, compressing them tight as the two floated higher in the cave.

"Over here," Katie spoke, guiding her friend.

Jessie popped her eyes open to be sure she headed in the right direction, then closed her eyes again to concentrate. The two floated silently to the edge of the upper cave. Katie reached out and helped the heavy warrior step onto solid rock again. Jessie opened her eyes, and landed lightly, her glittering feet softly shuffling against the rock.

Katie hugged Jessie and Alex, relieved that they now stood with her. It felt strange to hug the small, delicate elf and the muscular brute and think that she was hugging her best friend and her brother. They stood for a few minutes, grasping onto each other, not saying anything. Katie felt so guilty for leading Jessie and Alex into this game and causing them injury.

Katie gently released her brother and friend and then nodded to Jessie's shoulder and said, "Hopefully we can find some elixir. I'm so sorry, you guys. I never thought it would be like this. I only wanted to find out whose voice I heard."

"I did, too," Alex stated, his face serious and sincere. "I don't blame you for anything, Katie."

"Me neither," Jessie said. "You didn't force me. I wanted to play."

They fell silent again, and even though her brother and best friend assured her they held no animosity against her, Katie still felt sick to her stomach and very guilty.

At this point, she just wanted to get out of this game. But how? Should they go into the tunnel? Katie turned and looked down the passageway in which they stood. The tunnel ahead dissolved into darkness as it stretched away from the cavern filtered with sunlight. Why not? What did they have to lose?

"We need a torch," Katie stated as she turned back to the magical elf.

Jessie nodded in agreement and then she sprinkled a little magic dust into the palm of her hand and a glowing blue orb formed. It hovered up over the elf's right shoulder and lit their way as Katie led the three down the passage.

The air became colder as they left the sunshine behind. Not knowing what they might face next, Katie walked slowly and cautiously down the cool corridor.

"I wish we could exit this game," Jessie sighed wistfully as she shuffled her feet. "What do you think is happening? Why won't it show us the menus?"

"I don't know," Katie said. "It did this before, but Alex and I were able to get out without the key because we found a frame." When she said this, Katie realized that maybe they could escape through a white, rectangular frame, if one should materialize ahead of them.

An area of light began to expand ahead. It wasn't a frame, and Katie soon realized they simply neared the end of the tunnel. As they traveled closer, the archer heard the unmistakable sound of rushing water. Katie approached the opening carefully and peered beyond its edges. She squinted in the bright sunlight, held onto the curved wall of the opening and looked below its rim. Gray rocks angled this way and that, and at the base of the slope, a river roared, tumbling over boulders and rolling into pools of white water. She turned her head and looked up above where she stood. They were halfway down a rocky mountainside. Toward the top, the stones became smoother and formed the outer walls of the castle. It looked as if the castle had been carved or chiseled from the stone.

"The river is one of the worlds you can choose," Jessie spoke. "Maybe we're at the end of this level."

Katie glanced down to her left and right, but no meters had returned, and no frame hovered ahead of them.

"Who knows?" Alex wondered. "Maybe we do have to get the key."

"Should we go back and try to get it from the dragon?" Katie wondered warily. She turned her head back toward the dark passage and saw the worried faces of her two companions. The elf's thin brows furrowed slightly and the warrior held his strong, bearded jaw clenched tight.

Then Alex said, "I can't get close enough to strike it with my sword." He patted his sheathed weapon. "And I dropped my shield back there." He pointed over his shoulder with his head and looked a little embarrassed that he had dropped a weapon. "I only grabbed the grappling hook and rope," Alex said as he returned them to Katie.

"I only have two spells left," Jessie said, shaking her head.

"Fire and water," Katie said. "Water could put out a flame, but only one. Fire – well, that might shock it for a little while."

"Even the fireballs only seemed to have a little effect," Jessie conceded. "And I lost count. I don't know how many I have left."

"Normally we'd be able to see it in the display. Normally," Alex emphasized with raised brows.

Katie knew that her arrows had no effect on the dragon and the grappling hook and rope would not help. They couldn't face the dragon again.

"Maybe if we cross the river," Katie said as she looked back out and down to the foaming torrent below, "that will finish the level and we'll be able to see a frame and exit." She turned back to the magical elf. "Jessie, do you think you could fly all three of us down to the other side of the river?"

"I can try," the elf said, nodding. She pulled the black bag from under her belt and reached in for a handful of magic dust. She coated the tops of her shoes, cinched the velvet shut and tugged the bag tightly up under her belt. The pixie swallowed, then extended both arms. Katie stood to Jessie's right and wrapped her arm around the elf's waist, and the warrior did the same from Jessie's left. Jessie gripped them as well, and then she took a deep breath and closed her eyes.

Katie's breath quickened as her feet left solid rock and she floated through the air. They actually flew! The three gently drifted down past the vertical cliff, over the roaring, white-water river and landed safely on the other side. A small cloud of dirt puffed up as the three landed on the riverbank.

But Katie's exhilaration from flying quickly faded. Now what? Katie looked around and did not see any white frames or rectangles. She turned and squinted back up at the massive citadel. Small windows dotted the sides. The two corners visible to her were rounded and topped with stones placed in squared edges, some high, some low, like a square zigzag.

As she looked up toward the castle, Katie swallowed. Her throat felt dry and tight. She felt very thirsty. The archer marveled at the feeling. How could a game make her feel *thirsty?* At first the intense reality of the game had been fascinating, but now she found it irritating.

Katie felt compelled to take care of her thirst. She knelt down in the brown dirt by the side of the river and scooped up a palm full of the clear, cold water. She let the smooth fluid flow over her dry tongue and gulped it down her parched throat. Some dripped down over her chin and dropped onto her cloth tunic. Jessie and Alex followed her lead and both knelt by the water and drank.

"Ahh," Alex breathed. "Tastes good!"

"Yes, it does," Katie agreed, surprised and yet not so astounded by the wonderful flavor.

Katie rested back on her heels. The brute sat cross-legged and the elf leaned on her right arm with her knees curled together to her left. Now what should they do? Maybe they could get the key from the river world? The water ran very swiftly. If the key were somewhere downstream, they would need a raft of some sort to navigate the river. Where would they find a raft?

A breeze brushed past and ruffled Katie's short brown hair. The archer turned from the rushing waters and looked behind where she knelt. A meadow stretched from the riverbank to the edge of a forest. Many pines, leafy trees and green bushes grew in the glade. Were these the same woods where vines extended to grip you and marshes swallowed your legs? They had made it through the forest before; perhaps they could do it again, and this time find the key. Maybe once they'd found a key, they would be able to get out of the game.

Katie rose to her feet and stared into the woods, hands on her hips. Alex and Jessie stood up and walked to her side, frowning, peering in the same direction.

"Let's head into the forest," Katie suggested. "We know we can cut through the vines and swing over the marsh. We just need to figure out where the key is hidden."

"And if we find the key we can exit?" Jessie sounded hopeful, but hesitant, as if she wasn't sure they'd be able to get out.

"I hope so," Katie sighed. Then she thought twice about having the others go with her. She did not want to risk further harm to them. "I want you two to stay here. I'll go into the forest and get the key."

"No," Alex said, frowning and shaking his head.

"I don't want you to get hurt again," Katie explained.

"I'm bigger and stronger than you," the warrior said. "You need me to help."

"My shoulder is all right," Jessie said. "Besides, I have two spells left and a lot of magic dust."

"Dust!" Katie smacked her head. "I wonder if you could spread dust on the dragon and make it turn to stone or something."

"What was I thinking?" Jessie scolded herself. "It was so dark in there all I could think about was light."

"So, do we go back to the castle or go in there?" Alex motioned to the woods.

They fell silent for a few moments, each mulling over their options. Then Katie said, "I think it might be easier to go through the forest."

Alex nodded and stood next to the archer. "I think we should stick together so we can help each other out," Alex's deep voice rumbled.

"I agree," Jessie confirmed. "Stick together."

Katie nodded and, with relief and reluctance, she motioned for them all to hike into the woods.

10

The trio crossed the meadow – Katie out in front, the elf behind her and Alex bringing up the rear. Knee-high green and golden grasses, some with fuzzy caterpillar tops and some with separate small branches and tiny weed seeds tickled against her legs. Large thistles with their spiny pink flowers dotted the dale, as well as miniature daisies.

Katie paused at the edge of the trees. Was this the same forest that contained the vines and marsh? Or were these different woods with new obstacles? She loaded an arrow in her crossbow and drew the small blade from her waist.

As she turned back toward the other two, Katie warned them, "I think we should be ready for anything."

Jessie nodded and patted her book of spells and bag of magic dust. Alex removed his sword from its leather sheath and signaled readiness. Katie turned and took a deep breath as she cautiously stepped into the woods.

Large pines, maples and cottonwoods towered over them. Sunlight sprinkled over the three through the thick leaves and limbs overhead. Katie wove around large trunks, fallen trees and branches, rocks and small bushes. Through the soles of her boots she felt the hard rocks and soft grass.

Several different types of birds whistled and sang to each other. Katie saw their small shapes flit and flutter from branch to branch. The detail in this game truly amazed her. Whoever created it even included these small birds. Hopefully the birds wouldn't turn into something nasty.

Katie heard rustling and froze. It could be a chipmunk, a squirrel – or vines. The archer's gaze darted across the forest floor, watching for any motion among the leaves and bramble. Nothing moved except the occasional branch or foliage pushed by the gentle breezes. What could it be?

The archer looked at the two behind her. The elf's eyes grew wide with anticipation. The warrior held his sword in his right hand, across his body, ready to strike.

Katie, with her heartbeat in her ears, turned forward and walked cautiously through the forest ahead of the others. Crackling leaves softly crunched under her feet. She held her left arm out ahead of her and gripped the small knife in her right hand.

The glade thinned and thankfully they didn't run into any vines or bog. Ahead of them rose a small hill, covered with savannah grasses and flowers, and beyond it stretched more trees. Would the top of the hill be the entry point she was familiar with? If so, then maybe the next forest would contain the twines and bog. Or was this a different path, similar to what had happened in the castle? If it were, then perhaps, like the slowly sloping floor in the castle, it would lead them to the key.

The archer led the trio up the knoll. She stood at the crest and surveyed the area. Another forest appeared directly ahead, instead of to the right as it did in the familiar entry point. Where were they? Certainly they could not just wander around in this game. It had to have programmed "worlds" but seemed to let them trek off in any direction now. Frustrated and tired, Katie trudged on through the tall weeds as she wiped perspiration from her forehead.

Not knowing which way to go, Katie meandered back into the woods with her crossbow lowered and her knife back in its sheath. She didn't sense any dangers now. The others followed behind. In the shadows of the forest, the sweat on the archer's forehead turned cool and comforting.

They continued through the grove for a while. Time passed. Mom would be home first and might come looking for them in Katie's room. What would she think if she saw them standing like zombies? Maybe she would try to get the masks and gloves off and would set them free. Katie could only hope.

"Mom should be home soon," Alex called.

"I was just thinking the same thing," Katie agreed.

"Do you think she could disconnect us?" Alex wondered.

"I'm sure she'll try," Katie said as she stepped over a boulder.

"Do you think she'll be mad?" Alex asked, hesitation in his voice.

"I don't know," Katie said but she knew their mother would not understand why they were playing a game. Any scolding she received now she would gladly take just to be out of this game.

More time passed as they hiked along. It felt as though hours flew by. Mom did not snatch the masks from their faces and set them free. What was happening in the outside world? Did Mom not wonder where they were? What about Jessie's mom? She would be worried too, if Jessie did not come home. Did time only pass in here, in the game, while the outside world stood still?

With effort, Katie trudged up a steep incline. At the top of the rise she stopped and caught her breath. Jessie stepped up beside her to the right and Alex to the left, both of them also breathing heavily. They stood at the edge of a cliff, and below them Katie saw a steep drop. The gray rock of the hill lay exposed, as if sliced away. At the base of the precipice flowed a small sparkling stream.

Katie felt thirsty again. To her right, the hill tapered off slowly into a small ravine. The ravine emptied out into a grassy, sandy area near the stream. She led the other two down. They trekked through the small gully and out to the water's edge. The archer, elf and warrior knelt by the side of the creek and lifted palmfuls of water to their lips.

Katie rested and looked over their surroundings. They would need some sort of shelter for the night. She couldn't believe it. They'd have to spend the night in this game!

The sky opposite the cliff began to glow light yellow-orange and pink toward the horizon. Across the stream, more forest lay ahead. Perhaps tomorrow they would reach the vines. She looked behind her and spied a low, shallow cave tucked under the base of the stone ledge. Maybe they could sleep in there. She walked to the grotto and crouched, holding her left hand against the outside rock. Soft, fine sand covered the ground. The three of them could fit into the small area and comfortably spend the night.

She straightened up and turned to go back to the creek, but the others had quietly followed and stood behind her.

"We can sleep here," Katie said, motioning to the cave. Alex and Jessie agreed silently.

As the sun set, the air became crisp and chilly. Katie noticed that Jessie shivered slightly, yet she did not complain. Jessie always took everything in stride, good or bad. She didn't seem to let things bother her. Except Ty's death.

Where was Ty now? Katie felt even more foolish for believing that she would find him, or his spirit inside a virtual reality game. They had not heard the voice at all since they had entered the game that day.

"Let's gather some wood for a fire," Katie said, trying to redirect herself. Jessie shivered as she nodded to Katie, anxious to assist.

They trudged up and down the banks of the stream, collecting small logs and dry sticks. Each of them returned, with their arms full of wood and dumped the small logs into a pile in front of the cave. The wood made a hollow, clunking sound as it dropped onto the stack. Katie squatted and picked through the boughs and branches for good pieces of tinder. She stacked twigs and sticks like a teepee. As she worked, she noticed that goosebumps had formed on her arms. Their presence annoyed her. She had had enough of the realities of this game.

The archer stood and asked the elf, "Can you spare a fireball to light the fire?"

"Sure," Jessie said and stepped forward, linked her thumbs together and cupped her palms. A small yellow glow formed and grew within her hands. She then opened her fingers and a flaming ball shot away and immediately engulfed the dry wood.

Katie loaded small branches and logs onto the flames, and soon a large fire crackled and popped. Jessie knelt close and held out her arms to gather warmth in her fingers.

"What do we do now?" Alex exhaled with a sigh as he lowered himself to the ground. He sat cross-legged and looked at Katie.

"I don't know," Katie stated honestly. "We should sleep here for the night and then go on in the morning."

"Keep looking for a key?" The warrior asked and yawned.

"I don't know what else to do," Katie said and shrugged.

Alex nodded and stretched. He reached his right arm up behind him and scratched his back. Alex leaned to his side, still near the fire but partially under the overhang. He formed a pillow with his arms and rested his head. It seemed only seconds and the big brute breathed heavily, already asleep.

"What about the voice?' Jessie asked, not really wanting an answer. "I wish we'd hear it again."

Katie nodded, but did not say anything. Jessie sat to Katie's right. She seemed deep in thought.

"Katie," Jessie spoke quietly, her voice barely above a whisper. "I never told you this before but I've had a crush on Ty for years."

Katie did not know what to say. Not only did she find it interesting that Jessie should chose this particular moment for her confession, but she also wondered if she should embarrass her friend by saying that she knew. Katie decided to be honest, so she smiled at Jessie and nodded. "I know."

"You *know?*" Jessie asked.

"Yes," Katie replied, smiling kindly at her friend.

Jessie laughed lightly and shook her head. "Guess I couldn't hide it very well, huh?"

"Nope," Katie agreed with a slight chuckle.

They sat silently and watched the sparks in the fire. Then without saying anything more, Jessie crawled into the small recess. She lay on her side with her knees drawn up slightly and snuggled into the sand.

Did Jessie feel embarrassed? Katie hoped not. There wasn't any reason for her to be. Katie sat between the lightly breathing elf and snoring brute and watched the dancing flame and sparks. She placed a few more logs onto the fire. She decided to stay awake and watch for trouble – if any lurked in this part of the game.

As Jessie and Alex slept, Katie wondered if they slept on the outside too. Or did they just stand in the middle of her room, gloves and masks in place, not moving, like statues? Were they lying down on the carpet? Trying to make sense of it just gave Katie a headache.

The sun had set completely and as its light faded in the west, more and more bright stars shone in the darkness above. Katie stretched and searched the heavens for the moon, wondering if that detail would be present in this fake world as well. It was. A three-quarter moon rose up over the rock cliff and shone in the sky. Katie even heard crickets chirp.

An hour passed and Katie fought to keep her eyes open. Her head nodded forward and she jerked up and blinked. She finally succumbed to her fatigue and rolled onto her back, and then to her left side toward the fire. Katie looked up past the edge of the rock to the star-filled sky above. She nestled into the comfortable, soft grains of sand.

Katie's stomach grumbled. It had surprised her to feel thirsty and now she felt hungry. This game was so real! She actually did feel the slight weakness of hunger. The exhaustion of the day crept upon her, and she felt drained of all energy. The heat radiating from the fire relaxed her and soon she felt nothing as sleep overcame her.

11

Katie awoke just as the sky began to brighten. She lay on her side in the sand listening to the early morning chirp and chatter of the birds. Before she awoke fully, she felt like she was camping and almost forgot their predicament.

She rolled over onto her back and watched as, minute by minute, the sky gained light. She stretched and groaned. Her stomach soon followed, complaining of being hungry. She sat up and wondered what they should do for food.

Jessie rustled and stretched as the sun's rays lightened the world. The elf rolled over and greeted the archer, "G'morning." Then the pixie yawned.

"Jessie, do you think you can conjure up some food for us?" Katie asked hopefully.

"I can try," Jessie said.

Jessie stood and flipped the long blonde braid over her shoulder. Then she opened the black velvet bag and pinched some sparkling dust between her thumb and forefinger. She flung the gold flakes out over the sandy stream bank, closed her eyes, concentrating, and lifted her small, delicate chin toward the sky.

Beneath the gently falling dust, a large wooden table appeared with several platters of food. Katie sniffed the air and inhaled deeply the sweet scent of steaming pancakes and tangy smell of sizzling sausage. She salivated as she saw fluffy yellow eggs, crisp bacon and crunchy brown toast. All their breakfast favorites on one table!

Katie leaned down to wake the warrior, but the aromas had already lifted Alex from sleep. The brute sat up, rubbed his eyes sleepily and turned in the direction of the wonderful smells. He stood up quickly and walked with Katie and the elf over to the table. They slid into chairs and began stuffing their mouths with food.

The eggs tasted better than any Katie had ever eaten. The bacon was crunchy and crisp and the pancakes melted in her mouth. She remembered the cheese and bread she'd found in the castle during their earlier adventures. That cheese had tasted fresh and mellow — full of flavor, like the foods she ate now.

The game had given her the bag of food previously, but now it made them use some of Jessie's precious magic to create nourishment. Aside from food bags, Katie realized that she had not yet seen a blue bottle of healing elixir. Jessie could not be healed without the magic fluid. Katie thought it strange that the game withheld things it usually gave its players. The game certainly wasn't behaving normally anyway; why should the lack of food bags and elixir surprise her? Katie sighed and glanced down to her left and right. No menus or meters were displayed. At least the game allowed them to create things like this delicious breakfast.

Katie stood up and rubbed her full stomach. She walked over to the stream, bent down and scooped up a handful of the cool water. She felt energized, ready to face the day, and hoped the others felt the same way.

Jessie and Alex had left the table as well and drank from the creek. Katie turned back as she heard small noises. Brown, furry creatures with black stripes down their small backs scurried up the legs of the table. They grabbed bits of food and sat on their haunches munching, their small jaws moving in rapid motion. Reddish-brown squirrels with long, bushy tails scampered up and snatched bits of food as well. Birds fluttered to the wood and landed, hopped and pecked at crumbs, then flurried away.

Katie shook her head and looked away from the bizarre scene. She stood in the sand with the stream trickling at her feet. She stared out toward the glade on the other side of the creek, letting her stomach settle a bit and pondering their predicament. Where was the key?

"I think we need to keep searching each group of trees until we find the key," Katie thought aloud, and turned to look at her companions as she continued. "We can start with that forest." Katie pointed across the stream.

Jessie and Alex nodded in agreement and all three hopped over the creek. They crossed a short patch of weedy grass and headed into the woods. They crushed leaves and pine needles under their footfalls. Occasionally, a bird chirped or twittered. The sun filtered through the thick leaves and branches of the trees. When Katie passed through the patchy sunlight, it felt warm against her skin. The warmth irritated her. Katie scratched her forearm where the hot rays had tightened her skin.

Katie heard a loud rustling in the tree branches above their heads. She continued trudging along until the noise became even louder. She stopped and swept her left arm around, motioning for the other two to halt as well. She stared up into the thick branches and leaves and pine boughs that swayed overhead with the wind.

"Did you hear that?" she whispered to her companions.

"Yes," Jessie said, nodding her head as she too, stared up into the canopy.

Suddenly a flapping, flying creature dropped down out of the dark leaves and swooped over their heads. It had long, leathery wings, tiny, pointed ears and a small, mouse-like body – a bat! It passed over them, and Katie heard the bat make a soft screeching noise. As she watched it fly up toward the trees, the thick leaves rustled and several more of the creatures swooped down toward the three.

"Run!" Katie shouted and motioned for the other two to race ahead of her. She turned back toward the descending creatures and fired an arrow into the mass of flapping wings. The arrow hit nothing and sailed off into the trees beyond.

Katie turned to run again and quickly loaded another shaft into the crossbow. A bat swept low ahead of her and got tangled in Jessie's thick blonde braid. Jessie screamed and twirled about trying to pull the creature out of her hair. The velvet bag of magic dust flew from Jessie's waist to the ground, scattering precious dust into the dirt. Katie raced near to Jessie as the elf finally grabbed the wriggling thing and threw the bat to the ground. It scurried away into the underbrush.

As Katie reached down to pick up the black velvet bag, the pixie cupped her hands and aimed a fireball at the bushes. Twigs, branches and leaves flashed into red and orange flames. Then Jessie formed another glowing ball and shot it at the mass of wings flapping toward them. The fireball exploded with a sizzle and a few creatures dropped to the ground with small thuds and screeches.

Katie did not know if the dirt mixed with dust would ruin it, so she did not scoop the spilled speckles up, but simply cinched the bag tight and ran with Jessie and Alex, trying to get away from the flying creatures.

Alex swept his large sword up through the air, trying to strike the creatures down with his blade. One bat clawed his left shoulder as it swept past. Katie heard the warrior cry out in pain. She saw him cup his hand over his left shoulder and watched as blood seeped through his fingers.

Katie shot another arrow as two bats swooped down toward them. The crossbow on her arm vibrated with a hum as the shaft shot off toward the two creatures. The arrow zinged into the woods. Missed again!

The elf formed another fireball and shot it, hitting one of the two flying creatures and sending it screeching to the ground in a ball of flame. It sizzled and sent a stench into the air. The other creature flew away from them and retreated into the glade. The remaining bats disappeared into the thick leaves and branches of the woods.

Katie sprang into a run, racing away from the flying things and motioned to the others to follow. She led the way into the forest. The timber became thicker as she ran and she slowed to a trot as she pressed the branches and bushes out of her way. The limbs crowded in around her. She turned back toward the magical elf and the large warrior as they too noticed the limbs squeezing in around them.

Alex swept his broadsword through the boughs and worked his way up to where the archer stood.

"Is your arm all right?" Katie asked, nodding toward the blood on his left shoulder.

"Just a scratch," the warrior asserted confidently.

Alex took the lead and cleared the way, hacking through the sticks and branches. He struggled to swing his sword through the forest, creating a wake of broken boughs as the other two followed behind. Katie pulled her small knife from its sheath and hacked at smaller branches, but her blade could not cut through the limbs. She gave up, sheathed her weapon, and let Alex continue chopping.

As they struggled through the thick forest, Katie thought of something and wondered why she hadn't thought of it sooner.

"Can you fly above it?" Katie asked Jessie, while pushing a branch away from her face and handing the velvet bag back to the pixie.

Jessie paused and looked into the bag. "Most of the dust spilled out back there. There isn't that much left. It would take a lot to get all three of us off the ground," Jessie said, shaking her head and looking up into the canopy.

Katie agreed. It had taken a lot of dust to transport all three of them over the river. "Better save what you have left," Katie said. For now they were only in danger of scrapes and scratches from twigs and boughs.

The archer felt the branches close in behind her as they passed through. It was as if the forest closed off their retreat, sealing itself shut. Alex groaned with effort as he continued to chop and hack their way through the forest. With each strike, he expelled a groan.

Alex stopped for a moment, planted his sword tip into the ground and leaned on the weapon. He breathed heavily. Jessie and Katie halted behind him.

"What's wrong?" Jessie asked.

"Just…need…a…rest," the warrior panted. His face dripped with sweat, and droplets clung to the hair of his beard. Alex breathed deeply, then turned to continue in the same direction. He set his muscular shoulders and attacked the boughs once again. The warrior's large back twisted with each strike. His skin, visible through the burned gap in the back of his tunic, glistened with perspiration.

"Can you see a way out ahead of us?" Katie asked above the chimes of his sword.

Alex paused again and scanned the thick branches. He turned slowly back toward the archer and shook his head.

"Keep going," Katie said and pressed ahead as the forest encroached on them from behind.

Alex swung the sword again and chopped through the thick green branches.

"What if we're going in circles?" Jessie whispered.

She's right, Katie thought, but she did not say anything out loud. Because the forest closed in behind them, they couldn't tell whether they turned or went straight. The archer hoped that they weren't just winding tighter and tighter into the dense woods.

Ahead of Katie and Jessie, Alex stopped and breathed, "Wow."

"What?" Katie tried to look past him to see, but the thick greenery and his massive back blocked her view.

Alex did not answer, but swung the sword with new strength. After a few more strokes, Alex paused and said, "There." As he stepped through the branches, Katie saw a break in the thick woods.

Katie followed Alex and Jessie through the opening and stood in a clearing at the center of which glimmered a golden tree. Its huge trunk, numerous shining branches and shimmering leaves all twinkled with gold.

"The key!" Katie shouted.

Immediately the three spread out around the trunk and began to search. The archer scoured the smooth, shiny trunk, low branches and even craned her neck to search the limbs overhead, but could not see the key. She stepped around the base of the trunk, searching every crack in its golden bark. Katie met Alex and Jessie as they circled from the other way.

"Did you find it?" Hope lifted Katie's voice as she spoke to her companions.

"No," Jessie replied, frustrated.

"Nothing," Alex said as he leaned against the shimmering tree trunk.

As soon as he had finished speaking, a rumble sounded and a tremor trembled through the earth at their feet, making pebbles and dirt dance. With astonishment, Katie watched as a long, wide split opened up in the trunk of the golden tree.

Katie stepped over to the opening. Was it showing her the way? Or was it a trap?

She did not want to risk further injury to the others so she turned to the warrior and elf and said, "I'll go in. You two stay out here."

Alex and Jessie both made protests, but Katie stood her ground and said, "I don't want you guys to get hurt." The warrior and elf reluctantly nodded slowly in agreement.

Katie stared into the gleaming crack. Was she ready for this? If not now, when? Katie squeezed through the crack and found herself standing in a small room. A little light came into the chamber from the outside. She looked around and a tunnel leading away from the room extended to her right. Its opening glowed faintly. *The tunnel leads to a light,* Katie thought. *But what caused the light?* At least she'd be able to see where she was going. Katie got down on all fours and crawled into the small passage.

The tunnel surface felt smooth and sleek. She slipped easily along and noticed it dipped downward gradually.

At the end of the tunnel, she saw a chamber, and as she drew nearer she saw a small golden table in the center of the room. Katie peered out of the tunnel opening and saw a gold chain and key laying on the table. Katie twisted around in the tight tunnel to position her legs in front of her. Once she had gotten turned she extended her feet out of the hole and hopped out of the tunnel and onto the floor. She glanced around. The vault glowed brightly, but she could not see the source of the light. Only the small table stood in the empty chamber.

Why would the key be out in the open just sitting in the middle of a table? The archer cautiously slipped her feet across the smooth floor. She scanned the room, watching for any quick motions. She saw no danger, so she quickly stepped forward and swiped the key and chain. The archer stealthily slipped the necklace over her head.

Katie retreated and reached for the edge of the opening through which she had crawled. She wanted to get out of the chamber quickly. As she began pulling herself up, an uncomfortable feeling swept over her. Did something creep near, just behind her, ready to grasp her and pull her back? Katie sensed a presence of some sort. It felt like the same eerie, skin-crawling sensation she had encountered in the corridors of the castle. What was it? Who was it? If it was her brother, why did he sneak around?

"Hurry!" Jessie's voice screamed down the tunnel. "The crack is closing up!"

Katie quickly pulled herself up into the tunnel opening, and fear pressed her jittery arms and legs into rapid motion. As she scooted along, her breath became rapid and she scratched the smooth golden interior, desperate to pull herself along on anything. The entire tunnel trembled and rumbled. Would it close in on her? Did the smooth walls of the tunnel seem to be drawing tighter? Yes, Katie felt sure of it; the passage gradually shrank smaller. When she had gone down in the tunnel, the edges had not pressed in against her. Now she barely had enough room to move her shoulders and elbows as she clawed the sleek golden surface of the passage. If she didn't get out of there soon she would not be able to move at all. She'd be trapped!

"Hurry!" Jessie and Alex yelled, their voices slightly muffled but filled with urgency.

The opening loomed nearer and Katie frantically pulled herself along. The smooth sides of the tunnel formed themselves around her arms, back, hips and legs as the opening shrank. It seemed as if the tunnel did not want to let her go. She grasped the edge of the opening and pulled herself out of the constricting tunnel and into the small entry room. Quickly she stood on shaky legs and eased her right shoulder into the split in the golden tree's trunk. She held her breath and pushed her arm through, then felt Alex's strong hands grasp her arm and pull. Her shoulder felt like it would come out of its socket, and she cried out. Alex eased up, but continued to pull her through the crack. The split crushed in against her chest, but she squeezed through. As soon as she slipped free, the opening rolled closed and the solid trunk gleamed.

Katie breathed heavily and stared back at the shining bark. She had made it, but only barely. She sighed with relief but also trembled with fright. What would have happened if she had not made it out? She did not want to think about it. She felt the weight of the chain around her neck, grasped the key and happily held it out for the others to see.

"Got it," Katie said as she showed the warrior and elf, who

smiled with relief. Then Katie dropped the key to her chest. She glanced down to her left and right, but no words were displayed. Did they need all six keys? Aggravated, Katie spoke between clenched teeth, "But no menus." She slapped her hand to her thigh and then sighed. "Let's get out of here."

Alex looked around at the thick forest that surrounded the shimmering tree and asked, "Which way?"

They needed to see out above the trees to tell which way to go. Katie quickly grabbed a branch overhead and swung herself up until she could hook her leg over the limb and climb. She rose higher and higher, her body still shaky from the narrow escape in the trunk. She pulled up on the branches and slipped her hands over the sleek golden surface. The limbs felt smooth and warm against her palms. She climbed up, and up into the tree as far as she could until she at last saw above the leafy green canopy that surrounded the golden branches.

To her left, far off in the distance, she saw the castle atop the gray stone mountain. The forest extended to her right, but at the end of the glen sparkled the blue lake. Katie smiled. They could continue to the lake and get the next key. Slowly her grin faded. The forest between them and the glistening water had been groomed into a gigantic maze. They'd have to find their way through the labyrinth in order to get to the next level – the lake – and the next key.

Katie swore to herself. At the beginning of the game, when the game prompted them to choose a weapon, a compass had been one of the choices. At the time, she had thought it odd to include a compass as a "weapon." Now she wished she had one. Without it, she'd have to think of some other way to be sure they headed in the correct direction. She looked up to the sky and shaded her eyes from the glare.

The sun sat almost at mid-day height. In order to reach the lake they would have to travel away from the sun, to the west. Katie relaxed a bit; at least they could use the sun to guide them in the correct direction.

Next, she studied the maze. From her perch in the golden tree, Katie memorized the path they needed to follow. Unfortunately, she could not see all the way to the end of the labyrinth. If they could not find a way through it, she figured Alex could cut through to the other side toward the shimmering lake. If he had enough of his 100 strokes left.

Katie scrambled down the tree, twisting and swinging her legs out and down to the next branch. The limbs squeaked and slipped in her grip. In a few minutes she hung from the last limb and dropped to the ground.

"This way," the archer said and pointed to her right and ran to the edge of the thick woods. She then motioned for the huge brute to again take the lead.

Alex's sword clanged as it slashed through the thick leaves and branches. A few hefty swings and he had cut their way into the maze. They stepped into a pathway between ten-foot-high, groomed walls grown from some sort of thick bush with small, dark-green leaves.

Katie stepped in front of the others and shouted, "Follow me!"

She trotted forward and turned to the left. Katie followed the path, then she turned to the right. Perhaps this would be easier than she thought. She jogged down the long straight path and at the end turned left. She sprinted to the corner and turned left again, but ran straight into a bush wall. Katie backed away as Alex and Jessie shuffled up behind her. The archer blinked and frowned; she thought they had needed to turn left.

A deep roar vibrated through the bushes. Katie's heart leaped into her throat and her mouth turned dry. With resigned disbelief, Katie thought it sounded like the growl of a lion or tiger. The game couldn't just throw a confusing maze at them. It had to bring a huge cat into play!

"This way!" Katie shouted and urgently turned and ran to the right. She pushed Jessie ahead of her, then looked back to see Alex trotting, holding his sword as he ran. Katie did not see anything behind them, but a low rumble made her legs jittery with fright and sent her into a quicker stride. She glanced up at the sun as she ran. It would be in the center of the sky soon, and once it reached that position, she would not be able to tell which way they should continue. Only when the sun began to lower would the direction be clear, but they could not wait around with a lion prowling near.

They came to an intersection. To go west, they would need to cut a path through the thick hedges, or they could turn to either the right or left. Katie swallowed. Another growl sounded, this time closer. Which way should she turn? Katie shoved Jessie to the left and followed her; Alex ran behind. Katie wondered if she should ask Jessie to throw a fireball at whatever it was. She had lost count. How many did Jessie have left?

They ran down the path between the tall, green, leafy walls and came to a corner where they could only turn right. They swept around and slammed into a bush wall, and sticks pricked Katie's palms. There was no way out! Katie looked up to the sun and pointed to the bushes in front of her. "Here!" she yelled at Alex.

Alex swept his sword through the bushes. Leaves and small branches flew back toward Katie and Jessie as Alex cut a narrow path into the wall. Behind them, another rumbling roar fueled the warrior into a flurry of chops.

Katie loaded an arrow into her crossbow. Jessie linked her thumbs together and shot a fireball into the clearing behind them. Sticks, green leaves and twigs flew from the impact and flamed.

Jessie growled with irritation, angry that the fireball had fired. "I was trying to see if I could hold onto it," she said through gritted teeth.

The archer and elf stood next to each other and walked backward through the path Alex cut. They waited and watched, anticipating the inevitable appearance of the animal, and Katie peeked around behind her quickly to check on Alex's progress. It was slow going. Katie feared that, at any minute, the roaring creature would appear and leap at them, or Alex's 100 strikes would run out. She looked up at the sky again and confirmed that they headed in the right direction.

"Hurry!" Katie prodded the big warrior. Then she heard a growl so near Katie felt the pressure from it in the air. It was so close! They'd have to fight it right here in the confines of the path. Jessie cupped her palms, ready to create a fireball, and Katie raised her arm, finger extended, ready to curl toward her palm and send an arrow at whatever stalked them.

A full tawny mane came into view and with it, the narrow, focused eyes of a lion. The animal advanced slowly down the maze path toward the three. Its broad shoulders brushed up against the hedges on either side. Katie sucked in her breath. Would it pounce? For the moment, the lion contentedly paced closer and closer to the terrified archer and elf.

A fireball whooshed from Jessie's palms, but the lion ducked and the fireball flew above the lion, exploding into the bushes. The animal crouched and paused; he looked like he was prepared to spring. Katie held her hand out, ready to fire at the beast the second he pounced.

"We're through!" Alex shouted.

Katie's heart thumped. The lion's front paws left the ground. As if in slow motion, she leaned back and pulled the trigger by curling her finger to her palm and aimed at the lion as he leapt overhead. An arrow zinged from the crossbow. It shot into the blue sky, missing the beast completely. Katie fell against Jessie's back and knocked the elf to the ground. The archer saw the animal's long golden fur pass above her and immediately turned to see the lion land gracefully near the large warrior.

Alex backed away and splashed into a marsh near the edge of the lake. The lion stalked the warrior, carefully skulking nearer and nearer. Katie and Jessie scrambled to their feet.

Alex jabbed his sword toward the beast and turned to direct the lion into the quagmire. The lion stumbled into the water and roared. Then, the beast began to sink lower and lower and it forgot about Alex as fear filled its eyes. It thrashed as the water closed in around its shoulders and haunches. It pawed and clawed at the water before disappearing beneath the splash and ripple of the marsh.

Alex sprinted back toward Katie and Jessie, sloshing out of the marsh.

Katie hugged the warrior with relief. She felt embarrassed after she did it, but then felt glad that she hadn't held back. Alex had carved a path for them through the thick bushes and then chased the lion into the marsh. She smiled up at the large young man, but then looked down to her boots.

Katie realized that her feet had become wet and cold. The ground where they stood grew more and more swampy. In seconds, the water quickly crept up to her ankles. Katie searched the area to see how to get to solid ground. Only a few feet ahead of them, lily pads floated on the surface of the bog. The archer splashed through the water. She pulled her right foot awkwardly from the reeds and grasses in the marsh and stepped onto one of the broad leaves. The round foliage supported her.

"Get on the lily pads!" she shouted as she raised her left leg up onto another green leaf. Alex and Jessie waded through the wetlands until they found pads on which to stand. Katie sank down into the bog. The lily pad could not support her weight for long. She quickly leaped from one leaf to another toward the rocky shore of the lake. She glanced around her and saw that the warrior and elf hopped and jumped as well. Slight sloshes sounded as they sprang from one pad to another.

Over to her right, Katie saw the huge log that rested across the waterfall. The rocks before her were the same she and Alex had traveled over the other day. She steadied her footing, leaped onto the last two lily pads, and finally landed on solid rock. She turned expectantly as the warrior and pixie sloshed across the broad leaves. In a few moments, Alex and Jessie bounded from the pads to the rocks as well. Katie then carefully balanced on the jutting rock edges and smooth stones, climbing up until she and the others reached the sandy and pebbly shore.

The three stood staring out at the glistening lake as sunlight glinted off its waters. Katie soaked in the sun's warmth. She knew the key was on a chain around the lake creature's neck. She would have to go into the freezing water and lure the monster from its hiding place, wherever that may be, and then somehow get the key.

12

"The key is around a monster's neck," Katie explained to Jessie, "and the monster lives in the lake." Katie paused a moment. "The water is freezing. It would reduce your health and we don't have any elixir to heal you. You have to stay on shore."

Jessie looked ready to protest, but then her face fell and she nodded with reluctant agreement.

"You've been hurt, too," Katie said to Alex. "And we can't spare the dust to heal you. So I'll go after the key," Katie said.

Alex shook his head and insisted, "No. I can swim faster than you. We'll have to fight the lake thing together."

Alex looked adamant and Katie didn't want to argue. The brute could swim fast and she probably would need his help. The archer turned to the elf behind her.

"If you look like you're in trouble," Jessie assured Katie, "I'll shoot it with a fireball."

Katie nodded, turned back toward the lake and braced herself for the icy cold. She shuffled into the water. It shocked her feet, then numbed them, and she took in sharp breaths as, with each step, the water rose higher and higher on her legs.

"Watch out for the bees," Alex called to Jessie as he trudged beside his sister, into the lake.

Katie and Alex waded thigh high into the ice cold water. Katie peered down through the clear ripples. From here the lake bottom sloped drastically. They now had to submerge fully and swim.

"Ready?" the archer asked, looking up into the warrior's blue eyes.

"Ready," Alex said and nodded. He bounced up from where they stood, arched and dove under the surface. Katie followed. The freezing waters almost shocked the air from her lungs. The icy cold coated her skin as she dipped below the surface of the lake. She stroked up to the top again. Once her head popped up out of the waters, she gasped and looked for the large brute.

She saw his head emerge from the water and white spray fly from his lips. Katie swam out to where Alex surfaced. They treaded water, slowly moving their arms and legs.

"Do you think it will try to attack us?" Alex asked, shivering.

"That's what happened before," Katie said. She hoped that simply by being in the water, the creature would be lured near them.

"Wwwatch for it!" Alex stuttered with the cold and searched the surface.

Katie nodded and also scanned the lake. Smooth ripples spread out from the pair. She searched the glimmering surface of the lake for any signs of the beast. Ahead of her, a dome of water surged up, and slowly a large oblong head emerged.

"There it is!" Katie shouted and pointed.

Droplets trickled from its greenish-gray head as it rose from the lake. She saw the gold chain and key sparkling around its neck. Katie and Alex swam quickly in the direction of the monster. Its head and neck bobbed above the surface for a moment, then it submerged.

Katie and Alex stopped and watched the clear waters beneath them for the creature. The archer felt something brush past her left leg. She turned quickly and stared down into the crystal clear lake, but she saw only her legs. She looked back toward the warrior and as she did, something grabbed her right leg and tugged, jerking her down into the water. Cold washed over her, and she determinedly kicked and pulled herself up to the surface again.

"It's got me!" she gurgled to Alex.

The warrior swam toward Katie. He gripped the archer under her arms and attempted to pull her away from the monster, but the creature had a solid grip. It snatched Katie out of Alex's grasp and down under again.

The monster submerged and swam, forcing Katie to hold her breath. She struggled and desperately tried to pry the monster's webbed claw from her waist. The creature surfaced again, dragging Katie with it. As her head erupted from the water, Katie gasped for air. Then the creature hauled her along as it swam farther out into the lake. Katie saw Alex far off behind her, and in the distance, Jessie on the shore.

Jessie formed a fireball and shot it toward the lake monster's exposed head. The flaming orb flew out over the waters, its glow reflected in the surface of the lake. However, before it reached the creature, the fire dissipated and dissolved into the air. The monster was too far away.

The archer reached underwater, around the thing's slimy claw, to the small sheath at her belt. She pulled the knife loose and stabbed the monster's claw with all her might. Its grip loosened slightly, but then tightened again and the monster quit swimming. A dark-red fluid seeped from the wound and washed into the water.

Katie saw the creature turn its massive head and focus its black, beady eyes on her. Its gaze felt cold, removed, as if it didn't care what is had in its grasp. It drew her near its slowly opening mouth and a panic rose in Katie. Would it eat her? She screamed and wriggled and fought against the monster's hold.

She felt a current of water beneath them begin to pull them around. At first she thought it was another creature, but the force didn't yank her about or take her under. She and the monster drifted with the flow as it formed a lazy circle. They were caught in a whirlpool! The lake creature's webbed claw loosened from Katie's waist, and it looked around itself as if wondering what was happening.

The water began to spin faster. The monster looked around as if it was confused. Katie quickly scissor kicked to propel herself toward the monster's partially exposed neck. She snagged the gold key and sliced the chain that held it. The archer then gripped the key in her teeth.

"Katie!" Alex shouted above the swish of the water. "Tie your rope around an arrow and shoot it to me!"

Smart Alex! Katie had forgotten she still had the rope and grappling hook tied to her belt. But could she do it? Would she be able to shoot an arrow toward Alex without hurting him? Then could he pull her out of the swirling water without becoming trapped in it himself? Katie stuffed the key into her pants pocket and pulled the end of the rope from her belt.

Katie searched for Alex. The brute waved his arms while treading water. Katie watched him, quickly snapping her neck around as she spun in the swirl and fixed her gaze upon him once again. She fumbled with the rope under the water. Her numb fingers did not want to move and grip.

The lake creature seemed disinterested in her now. It turned and slithered to the edge of the whirlpool, trying to paddle its way out of the current, but the whirlpool's force kept it and Katie trapped inside its swirl.

Katie finally tied the end of the rope around an arrow and shakily loaded it in her crossbow. She blinked as the creature splashed water in her face. It became more frantic and desperate as it fought to escape the spinning torrent. She tried to kick away from the creature but could not. She scanned the shore for Alex again and once she saw him, she kept her eyes on him, aimed the arrow and let it fly. It shot off and away from her, plunging into the lake.

Missed again! Katie scolded herself silently just as one of the monster's giant arms came down on her shoulder and dragged her under the surface. She opened her eyes in the water and saw the clear, whirling tornado at the center of the whirlpool. She fought to reach the surface. She popped up briefly, long enough to catch a breath. But the whirlpool, now spinning even faster, sucked her and the monster under and into its vortex.

Soon, dots speckled Katie's vision. Weakly, she floundered about under the surface. She felt that consciousness would soon leave her, and wondered what would happen to her if she passed out. Game over? Real game over, she felt. Death. Her ears filled with the muffled water sound and the soft, slow thud of her own heartbeat.

She felt a tug at her waist and vaguely remembered that the grappling hook was still snagged through her belt. Weakness flowed through her from lack of air, and muffled bubbles floated around her face. Her arms and legs stiffened in the freezing water. She slowly turned her head, felt the rope pull taut and absently gripped onto it with her left hand. With sluggish movements she kicked to the surface, bobbed up and inhaled deeply.

She blinked and looked for Alex. Katie saw the large warrior being pulled along the edge of the whirlpool. *No! Not him, too!* Katie's mind screamed. She kicked as hard as she could against the churning water with her numb legs. The rope jerked and she felt herself yanked through the water. Another strong pull and at last Katie swam free of the swirling whirlpool. She relaxed and floated for a moment on her back. The warrior then pulled again on the rope and a small wave formed up over her shoulders as he hauled her away from the whirling water. She flipped over, paddled wearily toward Alex, and gripped his strong arm for support.

The lake creature cried out with a strange, frightened yowl as its head surfaced for a brief moment. Katie and Alex looked toward the monster as the whirlpool's spin tightened and pulled the monster down under. In a few seconds, the swirling water dissipated and not a trace of the creature could be seen. The two turned slowly away from the now unraveling whirlpool and focused on the shore.

Katie flailed her arms in half-strokes and weakly kicked toward the beach. Alex held her collar with his left hand and stroked with his right arm, hand cupped, drawing his palm toward his submerged chest. Slowly they made it to the shore and Jessie helped Alex drag Katie up out of the water.

Katie collapsed to the ground. She lay on her back and stared up at the sky. Pebbles on the shore pressed against her shoulder blades. She caught her breath and shivered from extreme cold. The archer slowly reached her right hand into her pocket and pulled out the key.

"I got the second key," Katie announced to the others, her voice quivering with her shivers.

Jessie smiled down to the archer, and then she knelt on the ground next to Katie.

Alex patted Katie on the shoulder. "Rest," the warrior told her. He nodded slowly and dropped to the pebbly beach as well. He sat, breathing heavily, water dripping from his long blond hair and light-brown beard. His helmet was gone — it must have washed off his head as he swam. His sword and sheath rested on the ground next to him, still attached to his waist.

As feeling gradually returned to her fingers, Katie unclasped the chain of the first key. She slid the second onto the gold links, and then she fastened the necklace securely about her neck.

Katie, Alex and Jessie rested in the hot sun and absorbed its warmth for quite a while. Katie had turned to her stomach to let her back dry. She relaxed with her arms folded on the sandy ground in front of her and her chin resting on the back of her hands.

What should they do next? If they continued around this side of the lake, they would encounter the bees. If they tried to avoid the swarm they would all end up in the freezing lake, soaked and cold. The lake monster seemed to be gone now, so maybe that was their best option. They could swim across the cove and be on their way with no danger from the creature. If they hiked down the opposite shore they would have to cross the waterfall using the splitting log. Which would be easiest? The game probably would make the log crack again. Who knows if one of them might end up going over the edge and down the waterfall?

Katie knew that Jessie still had two spells left – fire and water. Perhaps she could use one of the spells against the bees. If not, she did have some magic dust and maybe a few fireballs. Energized and encouraged, Katie pushed herself up to her knees.

"We're going to go up this way," she said, pointing along the shore.

"That's where the bees are," Alex said, frowning and seemed to wonder if Katie had forgotten about them.

"Yes, but Jessie still has a couple of spells left," Katie said, smiling slyly.

Alex nodded and his face relaxed into a grin.

They all stood, groaning and stretching. They traveled over the shore and Katie again felt the soft sand press through her boots against the soles of her feet. The sun shone brightly above, but it arced lower in the sky, nearing late afternoon. To their left, the edge of the woods extended along the shoreline. To their right the lake shimmered. Katie hoped they would not have to enter the freezing waters again.

Katie saw the yellow and black mass floating in the air ahead of them. As they drew nearer, they heard the buzz of a million tiny wings. Katie cautiously stepped closer, and the others stayed behind her.

"Wait until they start to move toward us, then douse them with water," Katie told Jessie. The bees did not swarm, and Katie wondered if they needed to be closer in order to attract the bees to them. She took small steps forward, her throat dry and her heart again thumping in her chest. She inched closer and suddenly the mass left their hovering space and flew directly toward the three. Jessie raced ahead of Katie and Alex.

"WATER!" Jessie shouted, holding the book of spells up with her arms extended.

A torrent of water appeared out of the air and flooded over the swarm, forcing hundreds of small yellow and black bodies to the ground. Katie, Jessie and Alex ran through the mud, avoiding the faintly buzzing insects. The poor bees struggled, wriggling in the mire.

Once they hopped past the bees, Katie led the three around the back of the lake's cove and out to the other side. The archer trekked up to the exact spot where previously the game had forced her to turn left, and she pivoted to the left and started up the hillside. Katie wished the white frame would appear again. However, she did not rest on that hope because still no menus were displayed.

Katie, Jessie and Alex hiked up the slope, walking over dry leaves, pine needles, stones and rocks. In a few minutes, they had reached the area where Katie thought the frame had hovered previously, but nothing floated in the air.

"I think this is the spot. Alex, do you remember?" Katie asked, frowning.

"I think you're right, I remember that bunch of blue flowers over there," Alex said as he pointed.

Katie nodded and walked around, searching. The edge of the frame had been almost invisible before; the full frame had not appeared until Katie had walked directly in front of it. She scanned the air, hoping desperately that the frame would reveal itself. After scouring the hillside she dejectedly sighed and stood with one hand on her hip. *Now what?* Katie thought. Should they go on or stay where they were?

The archer pressed her lips together and set her jaw. She decided they would continue up the hill. "This way," she called.

"And maybe we'll find the next level, and the next key."

"Do you think if we find all the keys we'll be able to exit?" Jessie asked.

"I'm not sure," Katie spoke over her shoulder. *I'm not sure of anything anymore.*

"What if it doesn't let us out?" Alex asked, a shade of fear in his voice.

"I don't know. We'll have to find another way out," Katie said, trying to sound encouraging and attempting to hide her own uncertainty. *Sooner or later, someone has got to notice that we're in my room and maybe they can figure out what went wrong with this game!*

Katie led them up the steep hill. The sun sat much lower in the sky. Soon the horizon would turn pink-orange and darkness would surround them. In a little while they would need some form of shelter.

Katie took account of their weapons as they hiked. Jessie had one spell and some magic dust left. She could not remember how many fireballs the elf still possessed. They could find a place to camp, and then use a fireball or the last spell to light a fire and keep themselves warm.

Katie halted to catch her breath again, exhausted and wondering where they should stop. She scanned the slope above them and saw a shadow. She squinted in the twilight and discerned a dark recess ahead, carved into the hillside.

"A cave," Katie breathed with relief but she hesitated. What if something lived in it? She hoped it would be empty.

They hurriedly climbed the rise. Katie loaded an arrow in her crossbow and stepped in front of the other two. She cautiously entered the cave and a moldy smell greeted her. The grotto smelled of musty, damp earth. As her eyes became accustomed to the darkness, she peered in a little farther and put her right hand up against the rough, rock wall. She slipped into the darker shadows of the cave, inspecting it. She briefly turned and noticed that Alex and Jessie followed quietly behind.

"I don't think there's anything in here," Katie said over her shoulder, although lack of light kept her from being certain. Then she turned around and said, "Let's get some wood for a fire."

In the rapidly advancing darkness, they quickly gathered as much dry, dead wood as they could carry. The air became chilly and Katie shivered as she grabbed small branches. They brought the sticks and logs back to the cave and piled them up, just inside the opening.

Katie constructed a teepee of sticks. "Jessie, can you make a fireball?" Katie asked.

Jessie linked her thumbs together and attempted to pull the power of fire from the air, but no small yellow glow formed in her cupped fingers. The elf concentrated and tried once again to create a fireball, but nothing happened.

"Must have used them all up." Jessie shrugged discouraged. "Should I use the last spell?"

"We have four more worlds ahead of us. We might need it," Alex suggested as his chin shuddered.

Katie knew he was right, but they also needed heat. Jessie had a little magic dust left.

"Should we use some magic dust to create blankets?" Katie thought out loud.

"Then we'd have to carry them. I'd have to conjure up some back packs, too," Jessie reasoned.

"We need heat," Katie said as she bit her lips. "But we need food, too. And you don't have that much dust left."

They remained silent for a few minutes, deep in thought. Then Katie said, "Go ahead, use the last spell. It can only create fire and we have more options with the dust."

Jessie nodded in agreement. She grabbed the book, held it up in front of her and shouted, "FIRE!"

The elf's final spell puffed onto the wood and the logs crackled with flames. The fire spread warmth and light throughout the small cavern. Katie searched the back recesses of the cave and found it empty; it would be safe for them to sleep. Katie's stomach growled and she knew the others must be starving, but at the moment, she did not want to use any more of Jessie's magic.

The crackling fire played a lullaby and soon Jessie and Alex fell asleep. Katie lay nearest the opening, with the other two on either side of the fire. Soon, she drifted to sleep in warmth and comfort, but did not dream.

13

A bone-chilling cold awoke Katie. She curled up tighter, clutching her arms. *The fire must have gone out.* However, light shone behind her eyelids. If the sun had already risen, why did it remain so cold? Katie popped her eyes open and glanced over to the cave opening. It seemed extremely bright outside. She got to her feet, quaking with cold, shuffled over to the cave entrance and stared in disbelief. A white, fluffy layer of snow covered the landscape and more flakes fell gracefully from the cold gray sky. Katie closed her eyes and sighed. Another challenge. Then she wondered, could this possibly be the snowy world? If it was, then where would the key be hidden?

Jessie coughed. Katie looked back to where the elf lay as Jessie stretched and sat up. She shivered and looked up to Katie.

"Snow," the archer said, motioning outside.

Jessie raised a hand to her head, slowly and wearily.

Alex grumbled and turned over. He opened his eyes and stared out the opening of the cave. "Don't tell me," he said.

"Okay, I won't," Katie said, smacking her hand on her thigh, frustrated with their situation. "Now, should we use the dust for food or for coats?" Which would be better?

"Coats would keep us warm," Jessie said, "But we need food for energy and strength."

"I'd rather have something to eat," Alex said as he rubbed his stomach. Katie chuckled to herself. The true Alex, an eating machine, peeked out from behind the warrior's bulk. Alex could put away four hamburgers and be hungry again in an hour. Of course he would prefer food.

"What if we quickly find the key and get out of this snowy world? Coats would be useless after this world and would be kind of a waste," Katie said, thinking aloud.

"I agree," Jessie said and pulled the bag from her waist. "I'll make some food."

"Something that will last, and maybe a pack to carry stuff in, too," Katie added.

Jessie sprinkled a tiny bit of dust over the ground in the cave. Some apples, jerky and bread appeared along with a backpack. "This is all I could think of. Hope it will be enough," Jessie said, shrugging. She handed Katie and Alex each an apple, kept one out for herself, and then Jessie placed everything else into the pack. The elf threaded her arms through the straps and shrugged her shoulders to adjust the pack on her back.

They ate the crisp apples quickly, stamping their feet to keep warm. Alex finished first, eating almost everything except the stem and seeds. Katie tossed the core of her apple to the ground and when Jessie finished hers, Katie said, "Let's get moving."

When she stepped out onto the cold snow, it made a soft crunching sound. Since they had found nothing downhill the day before, Katie turned and trudged up the steep slope, her arms clasped around her shoulders, trying to keep warm. Snow continued to fall and soon a brash wind tossed flakes around. A short distance later, Katie's toes began to freeze. She did not know how long the three of them could last in this horrible cold. She again thought about using Jessie's magic, but did not want to waste the elf's precious dust. They'd go as far as they could without using her magic to keep them warm.

Katie led the three up the hillside behind the cave. The slope gradually became less steep, making it easier for them to keep their footing in the slippery snow. The snow was only about four inches deep, light and fluffy, but also cold, wet and slick.

Katie stopped to rest and looked up to the sky. The sun's muted glow shown behind the gray, cloud-coated sky. She scanned the hillside ahead of them. In contrast to the white snow covering the mountain, a dark cave opening, lined with icicle teeth, loomed ahead. Could the key possibly be in there? If they went in, they would at least be away from the snow and they might be able to warm up for a little while.

Katie turned to look back down the mountainside. Jessie plodded up the hill, the waves of her short brown hair dusted with flakes.

As the elf drew nearer, Katie reached out and held Jessie's arm. Jessie looked up into the archer's eyes with a frown. The frown melted away into shock and surprise as the elf studied the archer's face.

"Your eyes...your eyes," Jessie stammered. "They're blue!"

"They are?" Katie frowned, surprised and then told her friend, "Yours are greenish-brown, like they normally are. And your hair is brown instead of blonde!" Katie studied her friend's face. The elf's features looked more like Jessie. She still had the pointed ears, but Jessie's normal freckles speckled the elf's cheeks.

"What's going on?" Katie looked down at her hands. They seemed to be like her own hands, not the hands of the archer. Katie and Jessie both turned toward the warrior as he lumbered up the hill. In place of golden locks, straight brown hair covered the brute's head.

Katie held Alex's arm as he passed by, and the warrior blinked wearily and mumbled, "What?"

Katie studied his face. Alex's brown eyes stared back and his face, now younger and rounder, did not have a beard.

"You look like Alex," Katie breathed in wonder.

The warrior stopped and stared at the archer's face. He raised an eyebrow and cautiously said, "You look like Katie."

Katie didn't understand it, and a shocked, fearful panic ran through her body. She shook with fright now rather than just with cold. What was happening to them? "Are we turning more into our real selves the longer we are trapped in this game?" Katie pondered aloud, knowing no one could answer.

The perfect chaos of that thought throbbed in her virtual head and she brought a hand to her face. Her hand felt real, yet she knew it wasn't, and her fingertips pressed against her virtual forehead. She could feel her finger's touch and it argued with her sanity.

"This is nuts!" Alex shouted, looking at his smaller, less muscular arms.

What should they do now? *Concentrate!* Katie shouted to herself and lowered her arm. *Focus. Focus on the keys.* "We've got to get out of here!" Katie swallowed hard and pointed to the gaping cave mouth. "We should keep looking for a key. If it isn't in there, we can at least get out of the snow for a while." Katie peered cautiously into the cave and said, "I hope there aren't any animals in there."

Alex nodded warily. He unsheathed his sword, but as he lifted his arm, the blade and hilt dissolved and disappeared. Alex held his fingers open and his jaw dropped. "I must have used all 100 strikes," Alex reasoned, disappointed.

"How many arrows do I have left?" Katie asked quickly, trying to look over her shoulder to the quiver on her back.

"Four," Jessie stated.

Faint relief drifted through the archer; at least they had some weapons left. She loaded a shaft shakily into the crossbow strapped to her left arm. Katie extended her shivering and trembling fingers out in front of her and gingerly touched the edge of the cave opening, careful not to dislodge a sharp icicle. She ducked under the frozen tips and stepped inside. Alex and Jessie followed.

A narrow ray of light filtered into the dark from the opening.

The archer inched along the cave wall, feeling the rough rocks as she crept along. She kept her left arm raised, crossbow at the ready, and touched the wall with her right hand as she continued. She slipped her numb feet across the frozen cave floor. Katie saw her breath steam from her nostrils.

As they advanced farther, a small glow appeared ahead of them. Closer to the illumination, Katie heard dripping. In the cracks and crags of the rock walls, tiny rivulets trickled. The surrounding air became warmer and the light and warmth seemed to beckon them. Soon, Katie no longer saw her breath, and the feeling painfully returned to her thawing toes, fingers and face.

Katie turned around one last curve and halted; she, Alex and Jessie stood dumbfounded, staring at a chamber filled with gold. Shiny gold coins, gold rings, sparkling gold chains and necklaces, bracelets, goblets, dishes, and trays littered the cavern. Everything imaginable filled the room, all made of glimmering gold. *How do we find the key in this mess? Is it even here?*

"We'll have to search for it," Katie sighed and started sifting through the clinking mass with her tender fingers.

After a few minutes of searching, a low rumble rolled through the cave. The smooth stone beneath their feet trembled momentarily. Katie stood still, but extended her arms out. Alex and Jessie froze as well and looked at each other. Katie warily scanned the cave ceiling and walls. The rumble definitely felt like an earthquake.

"Quickly," Katie said as she pointed to a clear area of the cave. "Pile up what we've searched through over here." After dropping handfuls of shimmering stuff, they quickly continued lifting and sifting through the clinking, clanking objects. The effort and warmth thawed out their frozen muscles. They searched as fast as they could for the elusive key.

Another rumble traveled through the cavern. Katie's heart jumped into her throat. She gulped and again cautiously examined the ceiling and cave walls. A crack had formed in the wall to her left!

"Hurry!" Katie urged the others.

Katie scooped up a handful of golden trinkets and let them filter through her warmed fingers and clink to the pile below. Again, another scoop, then one more, but nothing, no key! Another rumble sounded, this time with more force. They had to step to one side or the other to keep from falling to the floor. And the crack in the wall split wider.

Katie became more frantic, and so did the others, shaking through jingling handfuls. Katie bent over and shoveled the last of her items into the pile of things that had already been searched. She dug into more of the remaining mass.

She heard another rumble, this one longer and more intense. The crack gaped open and a split traveled from the wall to the floor. Some of the golden trinkets began to drop down into the rift in the floor.

"No!" Katie screamed, afraid that the key might drop into the rift. She fell to her knees and pulled a few items back out, but she tossed them down the crevasse as she discovered none of them was the precious key.

A low thunder grew into a loud roar and flooded through the cavern. The crack in the floor split wider and new shatters appeared in the ceiling and other walls. Katie stood up and looked around in disbelief at the hopelessness of their situation.

"I found it!" Jessie screeched excitedly.

Katie snapped her head around to see the key, resting against her friend's palm, the chain dangling down the back of her hand and swaying slightly.

"Great!" Katie smiled and laughed with relief. "Now let's get out of here!"

The floor underneath Jessie split open and she slipped down the edge with a shriek. Katie leapt forward, landing on her stomach with her arm outstretched. She grasped Jessie's wrist as Alex slid into place next to her. The entire cave shook violently and the ground rose up beneath them and began to splinter. Katie peeked over the edge, and saw Jessie hanging by one arm, her other arm flailing. The gold chain still swung in Jessie's firm grip.

Alex grabbed Jessie's loose hand and Katie urged, "Pull!"

The two stood and hauled Jessie easily up over the edge, while the cave trembled. A crack splintered off the gap that had swallowed Jessie, and Alex's foot slipped into it, but he shakily stepped back up out of its grasp and wavered, steadying himself.

"Run!" Katie shouted. She pushed Jessie ahead of her and grabbed her brother's arm. She shoved him behind Jessie and ran full speed back out into the cold cave. They had to get out before the cavern crumbled around them!

Jessie slipped on the trickling water where the snow had melted; Alex caught her and put her back on her feet.

"Faster! Hurry! Hurry!" Katie yelled as she pushed them both forward.

The floor became colder under her feet as they ran. They'd soon be back out into the snowy world. The cave quivered with terrible tremors and cracks split the walls, overhead and through the floor. A large fracture broke across the ground ahead of them. Jessie easily leaped over it and landed safely on the other side. Alex hesitated as the shuddering opened it wider.

"Don't stop! Jump!" Jessie shouted.

Alex stepped back a few paces and then jumped over the crevasse. But the chasm grew with every shake and tremble. Katie hopped backwards, and then ran as fast as she could, jumping up on her right foot and landing on the opposite edge with her left. She pinwheeled her arms as she lost her balance and almost fell back into the rift, but Alex grasped her belt and yanked her away from the ledge.

Katie stumbled, gripped her brother's shoulder and sighed, "Thanks." Then she ordered them forward, "Go, go, go!"

They ran through a few more twists and turns. The opening to the cave finally appeared ahead of them. The icicles ringing the entrance shook and quivered. A few broke loose and stuck into the soft snow below. They ducked and held their arms over their heads to protect themselves from the icicles as they exited.

A falling icicle pierced Katie's skin on her right shoulder. She cried out and slapped her hand over the gash, then lifted her fingers to reveal red blood seeping from the wound.

They emerged from the cave and out into the blizzard. The wind threw stinging flakes against their arms, legs and faces with blasts of frozen air. Katie's blonde hair flipped around her head with the changing direction of the gusting wind. She held her left hand over her right shoulder and stepped away from the cave opening, squinting and blinking as specks pelted her face.

The ground beneath them continued to shake and tremble and an accompanying hissing rush became louder and louder. Katie pivoted and stared back up the hill behind them in the direction of the noise. Avalanche!

A wave of harsh snow thudded against her hip and legs and lifted her up, carrying her with it. She saw it sweep the other two off their feet and envelop them up to their waists.

"Alex! Jessie!" Katie screamed to them. In her mind she pleaded with the game to not let them be crushed or buried in the snow!

The snow mass rushed down the mountainside, but Katie's torso remained above its tumbling clumps. She saw Alex's arms and head as he seemed to attempt to swim through the packed snow. Katie saw Jessie's exposed head and neck also. The avalanche seemed to be carrying them along on its crest.

A pine tree snapped off and the snow mass transported the top with it, littering needles as it went. *It snapped that large trunk so easily!* Katie thought. *Thank God it didn't snap our legs in two!* With a crack, the avalanche swept away another tree.

Katie stared fearfully down the hillside ahead of them. Below her, the lake sparkled and rippled. They would flow with the slide, over a rock outcropping and into the freezing lake. The drop looked to be about fifteen or twenty feet. Katie shouted a warning, but the rushing thunder of the snow mass drowned out her cries.

The avalanche slid out over the rock outcropping, carrying Katie with it. She kicked her legs free of the hard-packed snow, felt gravity lift her stomach and then drop it again as she plummeted through the air and down a short distance toward the lake. She saw Alex and Jessie fall as well, along with clods of snow and tumbling stones and tree trunks.

Rocks and clumps of snow hit the water first. Still falling toward the lake, Katie drew in a long breath, then plunged feet first into the icy water. The shock of freezing cold flashed through her body. Underwater, she heard the dim impacts of more clumps. She stroked back up and popped out of the water, searching frantically for the other two.

Katie flowed with the ripples away from the mass of snow, rocks, tree pieces and bushes that poured over the rock outcropping and into the lake. The freezing waves tossed and turned and surged toward the waterfall, carrying Katie with it. Katie saw Alex bob up ahead and Jessie emerge not too far behind him. They flowed in the direction of the log that formed a bridge – a bridge over the waterfall.

Katie swam as hard as she could with the current, hoping to get ahead of Jessie and Alex before the lake's waves pushed them over the edge. Treading water, Katie pulled an arrow from the quiver that had somehow remained strapped to her back. She struggled to get her frozen, shaking fingers to work and tied the rope around it. She placed the shaft in the crossbow and looked up. She planned to shoot the arrow into the log, hold herself in place and grab the other two. Then hopefully they would be able to climb up to safety.

She aimed the crossbow at the large trunk as the lake pushed her nearer. Alex flowed past her, out of range, the lake surge taking him with it. He turned back and swam against the flow of the water, but the lake shoved him over the edge of the waterfall. Katie and Jessie both screamed as his head disappeared over the rim. Katie raised her arm to shoot the arrow, but it was too late and the lake sucked her down. She watched the log and her last hope pass overhead. She felt the surge of water press her out over the brink. Katie felt the heavy pelting of the water and the sickening pull at the base of her stomach as she fell with the rush. Above her, she heard Jessie cry out and Katie knew her friend had been swept over as well. Katie held her breath as she plunged into the pool at the base of the falls. She dropped into the roiling white water. She stroked under the surface, trying to kick away from the plunging falls, but it pushed her down. Katie swam harder, each stroke keen with determination and powered from deep within.

Katie exploded through the surface and exhaled, spray erupting from her lips. She bobbed along with the flow of the river and twisted back around to look at the base of the falls for any sign of Jessie.

The river took Katie in its grip and slammed her left hip into a huge boulder. Katie cried out and squeezed her eyes with pain, winced and moved her numb arms under the water to hold her injured hip. She noticed that her left forearm was bare. Somehow the force of the waterfall had ripped the crossbow away. Numb and exhausted, Katie floated with the swift waters as they carried her away from the large boulder and farther downstream.

Katie scoured the white waters behind her for any sign of Jessie, then searched ahead for a glimpse of Alex. She saw neither of them. Where were they? Panicked and wildly fearful, Katie's heart skipped a beat, then thumped in her ears. No! She wouldn't believe Jessie and Alex had been pulled under! She did not want to think that they could be gone. Katie tried to kick against the current, but with each motion a sharp pang shot through her left leg. She barely had the strength to swim, and the river pulled her farther and farther away from the falls.

She brushed up against an overhanging branch, gripped it tightly and held on, fighting the tug of the rushing river. Her heart pounded in her throat as Katie realized something appeared in the water and drifted in her direction. She breathed shallowly. The floating thing wasn't moving or turning except with the flow of the river. As it came closer Katie realized it was clothing. Katie knew it with dread; it was the green tunic that Jessie wore. Katie hooked her right elbow through the branch and as the floating thing passed by her, she grabbed ahold. She pawed through the floating green material and grasped a handful of brown hair. She gently pulled the locks up and raised Jessie's face toward her. She immediately felt her friend's neck, then briefly wondered whether, as a virtual character, Jessie would have a pulse. Amazement filled Katie as she did indeed feel a throb under her fingers. Jessie had a pulse. Jessie coughed and sputtered but did not open her eyes. Katie leaned near her unconscious friend's mouth and felt Jessie's warm breath on her cold cheek. Jessie was breathing! Katie threaded her arm under her friend's armpits and hugged her close. She released the branch and the two rode the cascades. Katie kept Jessie's face up out of the water as best she could, but the splash and rolling flow of the river tossed them about. Katie stared through the torrents of white water down river, desperate now for any sign of Alex.

Ahead of her, against a large gray boulder, the water rushed in a foam. Within the white bubbles she thought she saw the brown cloth of Alex's clothing. Her heart sank with a heavy dread. Had her brother smashed up against the huge rock? Katie reached out with her left arm as she washed past, clenched onto the vest and dragged Alex away with them downstream.

They dipped down into the backward curl of a huge wave. Katie held her breath and slipped into the trough. The pressure of the two bodies and the whirl of water yanked her arms and tried to tear the others away from her grasp. Her muscles ached and strained from her shoulders to her hands. Pain shot through her left leg as she kicked determinedly away from the wash and out into the normal flow of the river again.

The water became calmer. Large boulders no longer disrupted its flow. Katie, Jessie and Alex flowed easily into the milder, smoother current of the river.

Katie pulled strength from weakness and kicked over to the shore. She rolled Jessie up onto the sandy bank, then hoisted her now normal-sized brother clear. Quickly, she knelt by her friend and checked her pulse again. Katie still felt a throb in her neck, and Jessie's chest rose and fell lightly. Katie turned to her left, to Alex, rolled him onto his back and checked his neck as well. A throb pressed against her fingertips: her brother did have a pulse. Relief flooded through Katie. She cupped her hand out over Alex's mouth and felt warm, weak breath against her cold palm. Alex struggled, coughed and sputtered. Katie gently turned him on his side as river water dribbled from his mouth. He gagged and spat up more fluid, then gasped for air. A few more coughs and he finally took air deep into his lungs. Katie rolled back onto her heels but winced as her hip twinged with pain. They had made it over the falls and down the river without serious injury.

To Katie's right, Jessie coughed and sat up. She smoothed her brown hair back and, with shocked and dazed eyes, she gazed at Katie.

"Oh, Katie!" Jessie said and held out her shivering arms.

Katie embraced her friend. Jessie started to sob and Katie's chin quivered as well. Katie could never hold back tears if she saw someone else crying. But she hated to cry.

"I want out of here!" Jessie sobbed.

"Me too, me too," Katie agreed, trying not to lose what little composure she had left.

Jessie pulled herself together and released Katie. She wiped her eyes with the green cloth of her tunic and mumbled an unnecessary apology. Jessie glanced up to Katie, paused and said with astonishment, "You look exactly like Katie now."

Katie raised her hand to her own face. She felt familiar features, traced the line of her thin eyebrows and slid her forefinger down to the tip of her nose. She no longer looked like nor was shaped like the older, larger archer woman. Her clothing fit loosely around her. She now had her normal sixteen-year-old body, her blonde hair and her own blue eyes, she guessed.

Jessie looked like her normal self as well. Brown, wavy hair topped her head and her eyes glowed greenish-brown. Jessie's clothes still fit her fairly well; she and the elf character shared the same petite size.

Katie then looked over to her resting brother. Alex lay on his back. His dark-brown hair glistened wet in the sunlight. His youthful, pale face shone bright. His chest, shoulders and arms seemed tiny compared to the huge warrior's. Katie knew how disappointed he would be when he woke up. For now her brother breathed in and out but remained motionless.

The realization that they now looked like themselves, although they remained trapped in this virtual world, sent shivers up Katie's spine. What was the game doing? With all her heart and soul, she wondered if the game would release them once they found all six keys. At least they had three.

Katie turned and whispered to Jessie, "Do you still have the key?"

Jessie nodded and patted her throat, then pulled the chain over her head and handed it to Katie. Katie fingered the cool metal, closed her eyes wearily and then slipped the chain around her neck.

Alex coughed again. He raised a weak arm up to his chest and throat. Then he blinked and looked up at Katie. He attempted to raise his head, but dropped it back down into the soft, pebbly sand.

Katie placed her left hand on his chest and said, "Rest now." Alex lowered his eyelids, lightly nodded and settled into the comfortable grains on the riverbank, closing his weary eyes.

"Why don't you rest, too?" Jessie told Katie.

"We should all rest," Katie sighed and Jessie smiled a comforting smile.

Jessie wrestled the pack from her shoulders and tossed it to the sand, then relaxed back onto the ground.

The quiver on Katie's back jostled with her movements, but no arrows rattled around. Katie removed the empty quiver and tossed it to the ground with a thud. The waterfall and river must have stolen her remaining arrows. She then rolled onto her back between the others and gazed wistfully up at the blue sky. Lying there reminded her of summer afternoons when Ty, Alex, Jessie and Katie would lie on their backs on their front lawn and gaze up at the slowly drifting clouds and imagine shapes in the wisps.

A few rippled clouds drifted overhead, carried on the high winds. At Katie's feet the river flowed swiftly. Above her head, a short distance from the edge of the river, trees — they looked like cottonwood, maybe some elm too — stood tall. Some small, grayish-brown birds cheeped and flashed from branch to branch and darted from tree to tree.

Katie found her thoughts drifting like the clouds in the sky. They could drink from the river so had no need to find water. Her stomach grumbled, reminding her that they would soon need food. Had the apples survived or were they now mush? The bread would be useless, wet and soaked. Maybe the jerky could still be eaten? How much dust did Jessie still have? They could use some to create a meal. Maybe they shouldn't use the dust. If they didn't, they would need to catch something to eat. Her only remaining weapon was the small knife. What a relief she still had it! Maybe they could make some sort of trap for a rabbit or squirrel. What was she thinking? She didn't know the first thing about cleaning a rabbit and honestly didn't think she could. She would worry about food later. Maybe there were berries in the woods. She sighed and closed her eyes. Fatigue drained her of all energy. Her thoughts drifted away and she soon succumbed to sleep.

14

The sun had risen to midday height. Their clothing, bulky and bulging, had dried in the sun's heat. Jessie's tunic still fit her fairly well. Katie's clothing was roomy, but she simply cinched her belt tighter. However, Alex's tunic hung to his knees, and his pants trailed on the sand. Katie trimmed the extra cloth from his trousers and he attempted to adjust their fit with his belt. The clothing still hung on him.

Katie told Alex to sit down. She had noticed his swollen shoulder as she worked on his tunic. Katie knelt by Alex, who sat cross-legged in the sand. The teenager examined the huge welt on her brother's right shoulder. Katie gently touched his puffy, red, abraded skin and Alex winced, sucking in a breath and scrunching up his face. Beneath the swollen skin, blue and dark purple shone through. Katie thought he must have slammed into that boulder where she'd found him. Katie lifted her brother's arm and rolled his shoulder; Alex grunted and groaned.

"You have a bad bruise," Katie announced, resting back on her heels. "At least it's not broken."

Alex nodded and massaged his arm.

Katie gently pressed the fingers of her left hand against the puffy skin beneath her pants. She would have a huge bruise on her hip as well, but she didn't speak about her injury to the others.

Katie turned to where Jessie sat. Jessie had a red mark on her right cheek, but otherwise looked fine.

"Are you okay, Jessie?" Katie asked her friend.

Jessie held her arms out and examined them, turning them palm up, then palm down. "Just a few scrapes, but I'll live."

"And your legs?" Katie could not see bruises through the black tights.

"They're fine. I'm okay." Jessie nodded, reassuring Katie.

Small miracles. Katie would take them. "Is there any magic dust left?" Katie asked pointing to the black velvet bag at Jessie's waist.

Jessie snagged the bag from under her belt, pulled it open and peered anxiously inside. "Not that much."

Katie glanced into the bag as well. "The river must have washed most of it away," Katie sighed, very disappointed. "Should we use what's left for healing?"

Jessie looked down to the pack at her left. She grabbed it and removed the smashed apples and liquid bread. "Looks like the jerky survived. But we need more food."

"We still have three more worlds to go through," Alex stated grimly.

Katie nodded. "Well, if we think we can go on with the injuries we've got, then we should save what little dust we have left."

"I think so, too," Jessie agreed. "And we should just eat what we've got left." She reached into the pack and gave each of them a piece of the salty, tough meat.

Alex ripped into the strip of jerky heartily, but Jessie bit off small chunks and chewed them quietly.

As Katie sat eating her share, she looked around them. Across from the sandy bank on which they sat flowed the swift river. A few paces downstream, red rock cliffs rose on both sides of the river, with the water channeled between. Behind them stretched a forest, thick with bushes and trees. The sun shone brightly. Katie relished the warmth; the icy snow and freezing waters of the lake and river remained a fresh memory. Katie rested her right arm on her knee and chewed and wondered, where in this world was the key hidden?

After swallowing her food, Katie rose to her feet and walked to the bank. The river lapped gently against the sand. She squatted and scooped palms full of the cold water up to her mouth, while Alex and Jessie did the same.

"I should have asked you to create a canteen a long time ago," Katie giggled nervously. "But we'll walk along the river for a while and can drink whenever we want."

Katie stood and surveyed the landscape and horizon. They would have the afternoon to search for the key. Then they would need shelter for the night. The river world was one of the levels in the game, so she felt they should follow the river to wherever it led.

Katie limped along the bank only a few steps ahead of the other two. The sandy pebbles crunched lightly under her boots. The swift river flowed to their left, and to their right, reedy bushes grew close to the water's edge. Katie pushed the bush branches aside and held them back so the other two could follow. A hawk screeched from above and Katie looked up to see its broad wings slice through the sky, tilting this way and that, and then skim above the high tops of the trees.

The nearer they got to the steep cliff walls, the rockier the river-bank became. Katie used the thick bushes to help her balance as she walked along the river's edge. Jessie and Alex grasped the reedy, skinny branches as well.

The plants thinned out as they approached the opening to the canyon. Only rocks and small boulders bordered the river. The trav-elers stepped carefully over the smooth stones at the side of the swift stream. Katie hoped that they would still have enough room to walk between the river and the cliff walls as they traveled along farther.

They hiked into the canyon. On both sides, the sheer, high cliffs rose. The rock shaded them and the air became much cooler. The center of the river flowed in the sunshine and glistened. At the moment, the waters moved smoothly, rapidly and quietly.

"Are you sure the key is in here?" Alex's voice echoed through the canyon.

"No. I'm not sure. But I think this is the best way to go," Katie sighed.

"My shoulder is killing me," Alex complained as he hopped to the next boulder.

"I'm sorry," Katie said and could not find any other words. She felt responsible for bringing Alex and Jessie into this and deeply regretted that he had been hurt. A sharp ache radiated from her left hip down into her thigh, each step a reminder of her own injury. Katie forced a cheery outlook and brightly stated, "Look, we find two more keys, then we get the final one from the dragon in the castle — and we're outta here."

"Where do you think the key is? Up in the rocks?" Alex motioned to all the rocky shelves and cracks above them.

Disheartened, Katie craned her neck and shook her head with disbelief. It would be nearly impossible to search all the little nooks and crannies.

Behind Katie, Jessie cried out.

"What happened?" Katie asked as she hopped back across rocks to where her friend stood bent at the waist, gripping her right ankle.

"I slipped off the edge of a rock and twisted my ankle." Jessie winced. She sounded angry with herself and frustrated.

Katie reached down and massaged Jessie's lower leg, feeling for any broken bones.

"It doesn't feel like it's broken," Katie stated, relieved, but it began to puff out quickly. "Let's get some cold water on it to keep the swelling down."

Katie wrapped her arm around Jessie's waist, and they hobbled over to the water's edge. Katie eased Jessie down to a smooth rock and removed Jessie's right shoe. She lowered Jessie's sore ankle – black tights and all – into the cold water.

Jessie sucked in air through her teeth as her foot sank into the freezing water.

Katie straightened and placed her hands on her hips. How much farther could Jessie go? Could she walk on her ankle at all? On either side of them rose steep, rocky canyon walls. The river took a left turn ahead of them, and she heard the distinct roar of white water. It sounded like they would not be able to travel much farther anyway.

"Alex, can you wait here with Jessie?" Katie asked as she looked ahead.

"Yeah," Alex sighed, and he sat heavily on a boulder near Jessie.

Katie hopped carefully from rock to rock along the bank. Each time she landed on her left leg she winced. She tried to ignore the pain, tried to think of anything, and everything else. The river hooked to the left, away from a sandy, pebbly beach. Katie followed the shore and the curve, her footsteps crunching in the gravel.

At the end of the turn stood a large boulder. Katie placed her right foot against the back of the solid rock, pushed off the ground with her left and grasped onto the top, pulling herself up with effort. The pain in her hip seared through her body. She winced and stood on the large stone and peered down over its edge. A narrow ravine squeezed the river between its rock walls. The water turned wild again, rushing over low stones, funneling between large boulders, hissing and roaring loudly. The three could not climb alongside the river any farther; the canyon walls dropped right down to the water's edge. Would they have to go back? But where was the key? Katie looked down the trail of the river as it sloped through the narrow channel. At the bottom, it forked into two streams and flowed on either side of a small island. A large cottonwood grew in the center of the isle.

A screech echoed down the canyon. Katie looked up and squinted against the harsh sunlight. She put her hand up to shade her eyes and saw a shape come out of the brightness. A large bird, possibly a hawk and maybe the same one she had seen earlier, flapped its wings slowly and swept down out of the sky. She saw something glitter. Could it be? Katie leaned forward as if the motion would draw her nearer to it. She could not see it in detail, but a golden chain was draped around the hawk's neck and from it something dangled. It must be the fourth key!

Katie dropped her arm to her side and blinked slowly, still watching the bird's flight. How in the world was she supposed to get the key from around the hawk's neck? They only had a little magic dust left. She couldn't toss her knife into the air and just hope it would hit the bird; besides she didn't want to hurt it.

As Katie stood slack-jawed, disbelief and frustration whittling away at her hope, the hawk floated gracefully and smoothly in the air. It then flapped its large wings, cupping them around its body and landed on a nest toward the top of the giant cottonwood. The hawk dipped its head and neck below the rim of the woven twigs. *It must be feeding its young,* Katie thought. She watched its head rise up, then Katie blinked and squinted. The chain no longer shimmered about the bird's throat. The hawk must have dropped it into the nest!

Katie felt relief that the bird no longer had the prize, but her happiness faded. How could she get down to the tree — to the nest? She could not hike along the river's edge because no shore existed. She could not sidestep along the sheer cliff walls because there were no cracks or splits in which she could climb.

She took a tiny cautious step toward the edge of the boulder and peered down over its ledge. The river rushed past, white and foamy, and tumbled over boulders. Was there enough water for the stream to carry her along with it? Katie could not believe her own thoughts. Body surf a white-water river? It descended gradually for about fifty feet, to where the island stood, then swept on either side of the sand-bar. If she made it down the falls, she'd have to pull herself from the fast current and up onto the island. She spied a long, crooked, exposed root dangling out into the water. The river tugged on it and pulled it out a bit until it resisted and sprang back, then tapped the surface of the surge. If she grabbed that thick root, she might — she better — be able to pull herself up onto the island.

With anticipation and trepidation, she shifted her feet. If she made it, then she would have to climb the tree. Climbing the tree would be the easy part. Katie smiled inwardly, but her glee quickly slipped away and she licked her lips. She took a deep breath, and with renewed determination and energy she hiked back to the others.

When she got near, Katie called, "I know where the key is!" Alex raised his head, stood up quickly and stepped toward Katie expectantly. His face glowed with hope and relief. Jessie twisted from her seated position and with bright, eager eyes she watched Katie approach. "Where is it?" Jessie asked, as Katie stepped up to them.

"In a nest, in a tree." She paused, stood with her hands on her hips, and looked back over her shoulder, panting slightly.

Jessie frowned, confused, and quickly looked around the treeless canyon. Katie answered her unspoken question. "The river curves that way," she pointed, "and drops about fifty feet. At the bottom is a small island with a tree, and the nest is in it. I'll go get it. You two stay here."

Katie quickly turned to go, but Jessie and Alex both protested sorely.

"I don't want you to get hurt worse than you already are," Katie said, trying to convince them. One look at the tumbling river and they would understand why she didn't want them to go with her, but would they allow her to ride down the river?

"We're going with you," Jessie said, wincing as she slipped her shoe back onto her foot and bravely stood on her sore ankle. Unsteady on her feet, she tried to hide her pain.

"Maybe we can help," Alex said and took a step toward his sister.

"No," Katie sighed deeply and shook her head. She looked over her shoulder, took a deep breath and then looked back to the others. She would have to tell them. She'd have to explain why they couldn't go along. Katie pressed her lips together and then spoke quietly. "To get to the key I'm going to have to ride down a rough part of the river and then climb a tree. You might get hurt worse, so I want you to stay here," Katie said and pointed to the shore.

The three fell silent. Then Jessie insisted, "We'll at least go as far as we can." She steadied herself, bit her lip and limped toward Katie.

Katie sighed and tipped her head in empathy for her friend. "Okay," Katie finally agreed, "but you have to wait at the top."

Katie hooked her arm around Jessie's shoulder and helped her balance from rock to rock. Alex bobbed eagerly ahead. He turned and shouted something back to them when he reached the narrow channel, but Katie could not hear him.

Jessie hobbled along, sometimes jostling against Katie's bruised hip. Katie bit her bottom lip trying to keep from crying out. In a few minutes they stood at the brink, next to the large boulder on which Katie had balanced earlier. From where they stood they could see down the rushing white water to the island.

"*That* tree?" Alex pointed with a stiff left arm at the cottonwood in the center of the sandbar.

"Yes, *that* tree," Katie affirmed, helping Jessie sit on the rocks.

Alex shook his head and slapped his arm down to his side. He looked at Katie incredulously. Jessie peered down as well and sighed heavily. Katie wanted to tell them that she realized how dangerous it would be to flow with the river. Did they understand that she wouldn't even try if she didn't have to? She looked into Jessie's eyes. Jessie looked frightened, uncertain and reluctant.

"I have to go," Katie said. Jessie nodded and lowered her fearful eyes. Alex looked scared for Katie. Katie wondered if he feared losing another sibling. Then she wondered what would happen if she did fail. She remembered the lake. Under the water she had felt as close to death as she could ever imagine. She did not want to feel that way again. She had to succeed!

Katie took a deep breath, then eased herself down one of the smaller boulders until her boots touched the surging cold water. Her toes chilled instantly. She stared down the path of the river and inwardly cringed, hoping beyond logic that she would not impact against a rock with her sore hip. She pressed her palms on the small boulder and held herself steady at the edge, watching the water glide over the rock below her and over her feet and down into a torrent of white rushing foam. *You can do this.* She gathered up her courage, and with a stern, determined face and short, quick breaths, she shoved herself into the wicked stream.

The icy water took her immediately and pulled her over the smooth surface of a rock, then dumped her into the white foam beneath it. She plunged under and bobbed back up again in time to gasp a breath and prepare herself for the next obstacle.

She had been on a white-water rafting trip with her mom, dad, and brothers last summer. The guide had said to keep your feet out in front of you to push off of rocks if you happened to slip overboard. Remembering this, Katie positioned her legs in front of her, knees cocked. The river twisted her and slammed her injured left hip against a boulder. Katie screamed with pain, but the roaring water drowned out her wail. She scraped past the stone, sliding along her left hip all the way and then dropped into another pool of foam. Again she dipped down and struggled to lift her mouth out of the churning water long enough to suck in a breath. The rush twisted her and she rammed into a stone, spine first. The impact knocked the breath out of her momentarily. Then the river sucked her into a tiny channel between two large boulders. Gasping, she fell backwards, sliding on her shoulder blades between the two rocks, the water so shallow there that she felt the hard stone grate against her clothing and skin. She tumbled out over the edge and sailed through the air, glimpsing the short drop before her. She hoped the pool was deep. Katie sucked in a breath and plunged into the icy water. Weakness flooded her now, and she struggled to get her legs back out in front of her, but the river tugged her this way and that, slamming her into rocks and boulders.

Wearily Katie paddled, twisting with the flow, then she spied the sandbar and tree ahead of her. She had made it down the falls! She drew new strength and courage from deep within the corners of her soul. *C'mon Katie, grab the root!* She set her jaw and pressed her teeth together. Ahead of her, the thick root from the massive tree arched out into the waterway. This would be her only chance; if she missed, she felt as if her strength would give out and she'd be washed downstream. She focused on the root, lifted her right arm from the water and linked the crook of her elbow through it as she passed. The river tugged at her legs, unwilling to let her go. With relief, Katie crossed her left arm over her right and grabbed the root, then released her right arm, gripped again and pulled herself up toward the sandy island. She continued along the crooked root until finally she drew herself up out of the swift water, rolled onto the beach and lay against the warm sand for just a moment, resting and catching her breath. She had done it. She had made it to the island. Before she allowed herself to sink into weakness, she stood, chilled, aching and dripping, and looked up to the others on the edge of the falls. Alex pumped his left arm up into the air with a clenched fist. Jessie, still seated on a boulder, waved both arms above her head. Katie smiled and waved back, encouraged by their exuberance. Now to get the key.

Katie stumbled toward the tree. Her left leg throbbed with intense pain and she struggled with each step. She reached the tree and supported herself on its trunk. She slowly looked up the trunk, studying its branches, guessing at which would support her weight. At least now she only had to gauge her own small frame and not the larger, heavier form of the archer woman.

The huge trunk bisected into two sides. She wedged her fingers into the split and scrambled up the base, then stood in the divided trunk. From there, she clenched a tree limb, swung her aching legs up and pulled herself onto the first branch. She groaned with effort and discomfort as she propelled herself up and up into the smaller limbs of the tree. She kept close to the thick trunk, using the smaller boughs as if they were rungs of a ladder. The large green leaves shaded her from the sun until she eased onto the higher, thinner limbs and out into the warm sunshine.

As she neared the top, the small branches swayed with her weight and the wind. *Just a little farther!* Above – only a foot away now – sat the large nest. She heard the faint cries of the young birds. Far away, the adult hawk screeched a warning. Katie spun her head around and up, looking for the creature, but could not see it. *Just stay where you are, Mama. I'm not going to hurt them.*

Katie quickly scrambled up the last few limbs and curved her arm up over her head and into the nest. She felt something fuzzy, then something hard and sharp – the tip of a tiny beak, she guessed. They felt so fragile! Katie imagined the babies wavering eagerly on their unsteady legs, mouths open to the sky waiting for their mother to drop food down into their throats. The little beaks tried to close around her fingers, but she easily pulled away. Katie searched the nest by touch, feeling for the smooth chain and trying to avoid the sharp beaks of the small hatchlings. Bony, frail wings bumped against her hand and she heard the young hawks' peeps. Sticks poked her wrist, palm and fingers, then she finally touched something smooth and cold. She pushed herself up on her toes and balanced in the tree, winced, and stretched to reach deep into the nest and grasp the chain and key. She hooked her fingers around the links and pulled the necklace out of the nest. *Finally!*

Katie held the shiny glittering gold in front of her and smiled, but the smile only lasted a second because the mother hawk swooped low and dug its sharp talons into the back of her right hand. Katie yelled in fear and agony and shook her hand to knock the bird loose. *Don't make me lose this key!* Katie kept her fingers clasped tightly around the chain, desperate not to drop her prize. The bird screeched and flapped its massive wings. It snapped its head and sharp beak, striking at her face. Katie ducked away and hooked her left arm around the strongest branch she could find. She braced herself and turned the back of her right hand toward the ground, tipping the hawk upside down. It pulled its pointy talons from her flesh and released her hand. The bird fell like a stone for a few feet, but expanded its wings with a whoosh and swooped up and away, shrieking.

Katie looked at her hand and sucked in a breath. Thin trails of red blood seeped from the puncture wounds and dripped down her raised arm toward her elbow — but she still held the necklace in her grip. With her left arm still hooked around a large branch, Katie opened the loop of the chain and draped it around her neck.

As quickly as she could, Katie climbed back down the branches. Pain shot through her right hand when she gripped the tree limbs. She extended her right leg down, feeling with her toes for a branch. She had to judge its size and strength by releasing some of her weight upon it. If it held, she would then lower her sore left leg and balance on the next bough. The rough bark pressed through her boots against the ball of her foot.

The hawk circled overhead and screeched. Would it attack her again? Katie tried to ignore it, but suddenly, from the corner of her eye, she saw it straighten out and dive toward her. Katie inhaled sharply and flipped the small, pliable limb she held with her left hand up into the bird's way. It flapped its wings around the branch and swooped over and away.

As she traveled down, the branches grew thicker and Katie easily found limbs to support her. She stretched from one to another, and soon the dense branches and foliage hid her from the hawk. *Now it can't get me.* Some relief flowed through her weary being. She glanced below and quickly looked back up; she hadn't realized how high she had climbed. Heights were not one of her favorite things and she still had about twenty-five feet to go. *You can do this. Just a little bit farther.* She closed her eyes briefly and pried confidence from her soul, then opened her eyes again and lifted her right leg back, out and down.

She peeked down again. A few more feet and she'd be able to reach the huge split in the trunk. *Almost there.* She lowered herself down those last inches, then wedged her left foot into the crack. She stuck her right foot onto the rough tree skin, let go of the branch above her, and gripped the edges of the bark with her aching fingertips. Her left hand held, but her injured right hand quivered; she would lose her grip shortly. Shakily, she slowly lowered herself down until she could jump the last distance. She then pushed herself away from the huge tree, kicked her legs out backwards and impacted heavily against the dusty ground. She winced and reached for her left leg as pain shot through her body, then she lost her balance and backpedaled roughly, kicking up puffs of brown dirt. She landed on her backside, briefly knocking her breath away.

Katie sat in the dirt and sand under the huge tree and caught her breath. Off in the distance, up to her left at the top of the narrow channel, she heard Alex and Jessie's faint cheers over the river's rush. She saw Alex jumping up and down with his left arm raised over his head. Jessie's high shouts of joy made Katie smile. Katie waved up to the others. Then she looked down to where the four identical golden keys rested against her cloth tunic.

"Two to go," Katie breathed.

Katie stood and brushed the soil from her legs. She smiled to herself and then looked back up toward the others. Her smile slowly faded as she gazed up the waterfall to where the other two stood. The river was too swift, too turbulent – she could never swim back up through the torrent and over the rocks. In her haste to obtain the fourth key, she had forgotten to plan for a return route. How would she get back up? She stared at the smooth, red canyon walls. The cracks in the stone were few and far between; she wouldn't be able to shimmy along them. Did she need to get back up to where the others were? Or could she hike farther along the river? Behind her, past the small isle, the river rushed ahead in the same wild manner, toppling over rocks and boulders wedged between the steep stone cliffs. No, she could not travel on down the river. She was trapped at the base of the falls! Weakness gripped her once again and her knees quivered and bent. She reached out into the air to steady herself as a wave of panic flooded over her. What could she do? Katie's head swam and the world quavered. She took a step to her right. Her head felt light and her arms and legs tingled. Katie shook with fear. What was happening to her? She looked around wide-eyed, but then her eyes narrowed as she saw tiny golden flecks of dust drifting around her, sparkling in the air. Her fear soon lifted away as she floated up from under the tree, out over the roaring river and up to the rocky ledge, landing safely and gently on the stones in front of Alex and Jessie.

Jessie lowered her arms and blinked her eyes open with effort. She brought her right hand to her chest as if a great deal of strength had left her, and swallowed before she said, "I thought you could use some help."

Katie took two steps over to her friend and embraced her with a grateful hug. "I thought I was trapped down there. I didn't know how I was going to get back up! Thank you!"

Alex stood next to Katie. "You did it," he chuckled happily, congratulating his sister. "You got the fourth key!"

"Yes, I did," Katie said as she released Jessie and grinned at her brother. Alex's brown eyes glowed with glee.

Jessie gently gripped Katie's hand and examined the puncture wounds saying, "That bird really got you."

"Yeah," Katie said, sucking in a breath through her teeth.

"I should heal it," Jessie said as she opened her velvet bag.

"How much is left?" Katie asked peering into the cloth. Only a few sparkles remained, stuck to the sides of the bag. "No," Katie sighed, "save what little is left. We may need it." She stepped over to the stream and lowered her injured hand beneath the surface. The cold water flowed red away from the wounds and soon numbed her throbbing hand. She dipped her left hand into the freezing water, and washed the streaks of blood from her right forearm. Alex fished the extra cloth cut from his tunic out of the backpack. He tore it into strips and handed them to Katie. As she applied the bandage, she studied their surroundings.

It is going to be dark soon, Katie thought. She estimated only an hour of daylight remained. If they retraced their steps and hiked back out of the ravine, would there be enough light left in the sky to avoid tripping over the rocks and stones? They would not be able to create a torch to guide their way or start a fire for heat.

Jessie adjusted herself, leaning onto her left leg, and then gingerly holding herself upright by balancing on the toe of her right foot. Katie exhaled slowly. She leaned down and touched her friend's puffy and swollen ankle; the bones on the sides were completely hidden. They would not be able to go very far. Katie's own leg throbbed with a deep, aching pain. Rocks and stones covered the ground. There was no place to lie down and rest, but she remembered the small beach they had crossed before arriving at the edge of the narrow channel. They could make it that far; it would only take minutes.

Her mind made up, Katie led the other two back along the river-bank. The three injured travelers hobbled along the tops of the smooth rocks. Katie tried to support Jessie. She wrapped her right arm around her friend's waist and Jessie gripped Katie's shoulder.

When they rounded the curve, the small beach spread out invitingly in front of them. Katie stopped and helped Jessie sit in the soft sand. Alex dropped to his knees and then flopped onto his stomach. Behind them rose the canyon walls, and ahead the river flowed swiftly.

Soon, the sun dipped behind the rock wall across the river, and the long shadow the stone barrier cast crept across the surface of the water as the sun sank. The sky above still reflected some of the remaining light of the day, but they would soon be in darkness.

The sun's light crept away and Katie thought the dark chased away the brightness. Katie sat with her back against the rock wall, with Jessie to her left. Alex lay to her right, stretched out on his back and staring up at the sky.

Katie gazed up to the heavens as well. Between the wall above them and the opposing cliff spread a swath of dark-blue sky. Soon, the sun had removed all traces of its light from the patch above them. Spots of light appeared brighter and brighter as darkness progressed.

"Do you think this is the canyon world?" Alex asked, tipping his head toward Katie.

"I don't know," Katie answered honestly, although the thought had crossed her mind. The next question he spoke was one she had already asked herself.

"Where do you think the key is?"

Katie looked down to Alex and pressed her lips together. She shrugged her shoulders and then said, "I don't know."

Alex lowered his head and fell silent.

Katie worried. With all of their injuries, would they be able to scale a rock wall? Exasperated and exhausted, Katie leaned her head back. She would not worry about it for the moment. Now she would rest.

A brilliant glow peered over the edge of the rocks above her. She watched as the moon, nearly full, appeared and shone with white light in the speckled, starry night sky. She listened to the night sounds. Mostly she heard the roar of the white water off to her right. The river in front of her flowed silently. Above them in the trees at the edge of the ravine she heard an owl hoot, and from the rocks and weeds around them came the chirrup of crickets. Too real. A great surge of anger and frustration welled up within her. She wanted to scream to the world to be quiet. She wanted this game to release them!

Alex breathed deeper now; he must have fallen asleep. Katie rested her head against the hard stone.

"Is he asleep?" Jessie whispered.

"I think so," Katie answered softly. "I wonder why we sleep in here? Jessie, have you had any dreams when you've slept?"

Jessie thought for a moment and then shook her head. "I don't think I have. Why?"

"I haven't either," Katie said. "I don't know why but it bugs me. This whole thing bugs me."

"Katie, why do you think this is happening? Do you really think it has something to do with Ty?" Jessie wondered aloud.

"I don't know. I want to believe he's still here with us. I guess I just can't accept that he's gone. Maybe I just convinced myself that I was hearing his voice." Katie paused and then continued, letting her thoughts flow from her lips. "People use the phrase going through a death in the family, like it implies that there's an end to it. What is at the end? Acceptance?"

Jessie remained quiet but nodded.

"You said you had a crush on Ty?" Katie asked, not really knowing why this question came out right at this moment.

"Yes," Jessie replied immediately. Then she leaned toward Katie the way someone does when they are going to reveal a secret. "I wanted Ty to like me – as a girlfriend. Kinda silly, huh? I'm too short. Not pretty."

"You're cute!" Katie assured her friend. Jessie smiled but looked like she didn't believe Katie. Katie said, "I think it was just that he, you know, only wanted to go out with girls his age."

Katie fell quiet again for a few moments. She remembered Ty's gentle smile. She remembered crawling under the bush in the back yard with Ty when they were only six and eight. They crept into their favorite hiding place under the huge bush. She remembered purple popsicles in summer heat. She had so many memories of him, and the pastor had said to cherish them. Then she continued speaking quietly. "It's so hard. I mean, I want to accept it, but I can't. It hurts so much. It hurts too much, like pain all through your body without any bleeding."

"I wish I knew the answer. I wish I knew how to make the pain go away. I'm sorry Katie. I hope what I'm saying doesn't upset you. I don't really know what to say," Jessie said, her voice low and thick. She was almost in tears.

"No, nothing you could say would upset me. And I like being able to talk about anything with you, Jessie." Katie's chin quivered. Jessie smiled and her eyes glistened with the beginnings of tears. *Don't cry, Jessie.* Katie thought, trying to keep herself from sobbing. "And I know you're hurting too, and you miss him," Katie whispered.

Then they fell silent. Jessie lowered herself to the soft sand and curled up on her side. Jessie yawned deeply. "I'm so *tired,*" she said, her tone implying that she could fight it no longer.

"Go ahead and sleep. I can't right now," Katie spoke quietly.

"Okay," Jessie exhaled slowly.

In minutes, Jessie's sighs became heavier and deeper.

Katie sat in the darkness and listened to Alex and Jessie's breathing. Out of the shadows that embraced her crept the uncomfortable, eerie feeling that someone watched them. She felt the hairs on the back of her neck rise. Her heart began to thump heavily and her breath quickened. She moved nothing except her eyes, afraid to draw attention to herself. Only the brightness of the moon lit her surroundings. Katie's eyes darted from one shadow to the next, anxiously watching for any flicker of motion. She searched the silhouettes of the rocks and cliffs for any movement. She saw nothing and heard nothing except the pulsing of her own heart in her ears. What was it? Was something out there?

It was the same creepy feeling that had occurred previously in the game. She sensed a consciousness, a presence, but she could not see anything. Whatever it was, it observed them and seemed to hover out of sight, which maddened Katie. It made her angry to think that, if it was her brother's spirit, he was remaining out of reach. Why? If it was something or someone else, what was it doing? She wanted to yell at it to leave them alone. As she sat breathing short and shallow breaths, the feeling gradually faded away. Katie filled her lungs deeper and hesitantly relaxed.

Katie's muscles felt tense, tight and sore. She hadn't realized it until now, but when the feeling had approached, she had stiffened. She tried to shift and stretch without disturbing the others, but found it difficult. She settled for a few small twists and flexes and shifted herself into the sand.

A light, cool breeze combed through the gully. Katie shivered. She closed her eyes, felt the wind's cold kiss on her face, and hoped the chill would not rouse the others.

Katie tried to keep herself awake a little longer. She thought about the times they had played together — the happy times. She remembered long summer days at the park, swinging and digging in the sand. It reminded her of being young and just playing. Did they play games now to try to recapture that innocence? Katie wasn't sure, but she knew she would never get it back. She had lost some of it just by growing up, but more deeply and certainly she knew she had lost it completely when her brother had died. Not only was he gone from her forever, but gone too was the true soulful freedom of being young with no worries or troubles. She would only be able to grasp it now in snatches and bits stolen from warm summer days and sand castles at the lake.

15

Light and warmth coaxed Katie from sleep. She blinked and slowly looked around. She tipped her head from side to side, popping her muscles to ease the incredible soreness in her neck. Katie's lower back ached and her hip throbbed.

"Time to get up and get moving," she said as she gently shook the others awake.

Jessie sat up and yawned, stretching her arms up and out in front of her. Alex rose and blinked. Katie stood unsteadily, staggered a few steps, stopped and rubbed her back. Then she shuffled up to the river's edge and lifted a palm full of cold water to her lips. She turned and walked back to Alex and Jessie; the mobility was gradually returning to her limbs.

Alex stood and twisted at the waist. He raised his less injured left arm above his head in a stretch. Jessie brushed the sand from her black tights and green tunic, and limped on her right ankle. Katie motioned for them to come close and reached into the pack for some food.

A rumble traveled beneath the ground and shook rocks loose from the cliff. Katie protectively grabbed the others and shoved them in toward the wall so falling stones would not hit them. The trembling continued for a few moments. Katie stood with her back against the wall, wide-eyed. *What now?* To her left, she saw a huge mass of rocks tumble down into the canyon and river. Red stones of varying sizes piled up higher and higher until they stopped the flow of water. All that remained of the fierce river was a slight glistening trickle that flowed out from beneath the rock pile. Slowly the rumbling quit and the canyon fell into a strange silence because the river no longer gurgled or roared with white water.

Katie stepped carefully away from the cliff and stared incredulously at the dam that had formed. The obstruction in the valley began to creak and groan. Between rocks, water seeped and oozed and some smaller stones rolled down and splashed into the muddy river basin.

"Oh, no," Katie spoke in a long, exhaled breath. The dam looked like it wouldn't hold, and if the blocked up water broke through, it would sweep them away! She quickly turned and scanned the cliff. Above them, there were places where someone could climb, unlike the narrow canyon where the water had worn the rock smooth.

"The dam might break and release a flood. We've got to go up." Katie nodded toward the cliff. Jessie's eyes showed fear and worry, then determination. If she feared her ankle wouldn't hold her, she convinced herself it would in those few seconds. Alex bit his lip and nodded with quiet courage. Katie said, "Watch me and follow where I put my hands and feet."

Katie carefully crammed her fingers into small crevasses between the cool rocks and slipped her toes into cracks. She then pushed up with her legs and pulled with her arms, straining her muscles, aching hip and throbbing hand. She quickly searched out new indentations with her toes and fingers and continued up the side. She heard the efforts of Alex and Jessie and paused for a moment to look down. Jessie hung directly below and looked up when Katie stopped. Jessie grimaced and shifted weight from her injured ankle, but looked anxious to continue. Alex groaned when he gripped rock edges and pulled up with his right shoulder. Katie worried, but she knew they wouldn't quit anymore than she would.

Up the canyon, the dam shifted and a few larger rocks rolled down and splashed into the muddy riverbed. The grinding rocks drew Katie's attention from her ascent to the leaking dam. Where the rocks had fallen out of place, a small bit of the river's force poured through. If the entire thing collapsed and released the enormous volume of water, they would be swept away; they still were not out of range. Katie quickened her pace as the dam groaned.

Sweat coated Katie's forehead and neck. Her fingers shook and trembled but held, and her elbows and arms twitched and strained. Her knees and ankles flexed and shuddered. *I feel so weak. I don't think I can go on much farther. But I have to go on!* Each effort forced a groan out of Katie's parched throat. Jessie and Alex gasped and panted below her.

Katie reached up to grip a crack above and her hand slipped off the edge, pulling pebbles and dust down toward her eyes. She lowered her head to protect her eyes. Her left leg slipped; she had already removed it from its spot and now had to quickly jam it into any space to balance herself. She sucked in a short breath, then looked down into the upturned faces below her and saw fear, worry and concern. She shifted her hands and toes to get a better grip on her position. She took a couple of determined breaths and continued up. Somehow she kept her grip with her scraped, raw fingers. Her hand throbbed where the hawk had punctured the skin. Her feet ached; the thin boots did not protect her from the roughness of the rock. She felt every sharp rock edge through the soles.

As she climbed, Katie noticed a small tree to her left, growing out of the rock face. She paid it no attention at first but as she struggled to find a good handhold, she saw something through its leaves. Something glittered. Dewdrops on a branch? She paused and squinted for a better look. A breeze ruffled the green leaves, exposing a gold chain and key twisted around the small trunk.

The fifth key! Katie's breath quickened even more. She paused and studied the route she'd have to take to get to the tree. She would have to continue up about ten feet and then travel over to the left almost the same distance, finding handholds and footholds along the way. She did not want the others to follow her. Luck had graced them so far, but she did not want to take a chance that they might lose their grip and fall back into the ravine. Katie paused and steadied herself, then looked below, concentrating on Jessie and Alex. She tried not to notice how high up they had already climbed.

"Jessie, Alex," Katie said. The others stopped and looked up. The wind ruffled Jessie's wavy hair and fingered Alex's. Their raised faces strained tight and drawn with anxiety and anticipation. "That tree," Katie said as she motioned sideways with her head. "The key is inside it. I'm going to go get it. I want you guys to keep going up."

Jessie said nothing but her face showed several different expressions within a few seconds. Katie saw her eyes relax with relief that they had found the fifth key, then tense and grow wide with the realization that Katie would risk climbing farther to retrieve it. Her brows slightly furrowed with empathy and fear for her friend. Jessie reluctantly and sheepishly nodded and looked away from Katie. Perhaps she knew that her own injured ankle wouldn't allow her to go after the key herself.

Alex stared up at Katie, his expression a mixture of relief and anxiety as well. He nodded slowly.

Katie started off to the left, toward the tree, and Jessie continued climbing up, with Alex behind her.

In the canyon, the dam shifted and groaned. More water flowed from the gaps between the rocks. Soon the others would be out of range, but Katie could be swept away by floodwaters if she didn't hurry.

Katie tried a diagonal route, climbing up and over at the same time. She found some handholds and footholds, but sometimes she either had to continue straight up or only to the side. She went as quickly as she could without losing her grip on the rocks and cracks.

She watched Jessie reach the top ledge, curl up over the edge, and roll away from the rim. Jessie twisted quickly around and lay on her stomach. She extended both arms over for Alex to grab. Alex climbed the last few feet and reached for Jessie's arms, and she hauled him up over the side. They were safe! Katie released a quick sigh of relief and concentrated her efforts. She cocked her left leg and propelled herself up.

A few minutes later, Katie balanced next to the tree, reached into its branches and tried to pull the key free. She closed her hand around the chain and tugged, already looking above her for a good path to climb away, but the chain did not come loose. Katie looked back down and saw that the loop of the links wrapped around the small trunk.

She tried to slip the fingers of her left hand up to the clasp, but then paused. It would be difficult to unclasp the chain one-handed, and even more difficult to keep it from slipping out of her fingers and down to the valley floor below. How could she get it off the tree? While precariously balancing on the rock face, she reached over to the tree and began breaking off tiny boughs between her thumb and forefinger.

With a crumbling rumble, a portion of the dam broke away, allowing a surging rush to flow from its gap. The water pushed more and more boulders out of its way. Soon the whole thing might give way! Katie hurriedly snapped the twigs and finally scooped the loop up, out and over the top of the tree. She draped the chain over her head, relieved to have the fifth key in her possession, but needed to get clear. She scrambled and clambered up the cliff just as the dam completely collapsed and a great wave of water gushed through. In a flash, the torrent filled the canyon and swept past her feet, tugging at them and trying to take her with it. She quickly stepped up and away from the water, but it rose fast and chased her up the side. She saw Jessie and Alex above her on their stomachs, leaning their arms out for her to grasp.

"No!" she shouted. She would not risk pulling either of them over the side. Katie shook her head and motioned for them to get back, but they didn't. As the water surged higher, she grasped the edge, felt a rock, and hooked her fingers over it with help from Jessie. She strained and shakily pulled herself up, trying to get her waist and hips over the edge. With great effort, and help from Alex and Jessie, she rolled up over the ledge and onto the dirt. She made it! Katie lay on her back gasping, staring up at the treetops, blue sky and white clouds. Then Alex and Jessie's faces came into view. They both smiled and then knelt on either side of Katie.

"You did it," Alex said, grinning broadly.

"You got the fifth key," Jessie sighed and patted her friend on the shoulder.

"Yeah, one more to go." Katie closed her eyes and caught her breath. She did not know how they would fight the dragon. Jessie had no spells left and maybe only a little dust. Katie touched the leather sheath at her waist. She still had her knife, but they could never get close enough to the dragon to strike it. It shot flames several feet long from its jaws. Somehow they would have to distract it, and perhaps Katie could climb on its back and cut the chain from its neck.

She wasn't going to worry about that now. She needed to rest. Her parched throat complained. She tried to gather as much moisture from the inside of her mouth as possible and swallow, but it was a dry, harsh gulp.

Katie felt a bit dizzy and faint. The effort of climbing up the cliff had weakened her and she knew they needed food. She motioned for the pack; at least Alex had had the presence of mind to grab it before they had started their ascent. Alex wrestled the pack from his back and removed some of the tough meat. Katie knew the salty meat would make her thirstier, but she also knew they should eat to gain some strength. They still had a long way to go. Alex offered some jerky to Katie and Jessie, then took a strip for himself.

After a few minutes, Katie stood up and walked to the crest of the canyon. She looked down and saw that the river had returned to its normal level. It snaked between the narrow walls and rushed and rolled over the strewn boulders. Unfortunately, now the water flowed out of reach; they could not get a drink.

She turned away and walked back to where the others sat. She put her hands on her hips and exhaled deeply. Was she ready for this? Ready or not, they had to go on. Alex got to his feet and Jessie stood up as well, although she favored her right ankle; both looked eager and resolved.

Katie studied the position of the sun in the sky to determine direction. It was still early in the morning and the sun's beams trickled through the boughs and limbs of the pine and fir trees in the forest. As the sun's warm rays embraced the dew in the shadows of the forest, the drops transformed into steamy, ghost-like fog and rose from the earth. Some of the mist clung to the needles, and Katie thought it looked like a cotton ball had been drawn across the tops of the trees and left behind some of its fibers. Katie stared toward the sun. It marked east – the direction they needed to take in order to reach the castle.

"We need to go that way," Katie announced, pointing. "Are you guys ready?"

"Yep," Alex stated, nodding.

"Yeah," Jessie agreed and limped gingerly toward Katie.

"Let's go." Katie pursed her lips. She thought her own voice sounded unsure and she hoped the others hadn't noticed.

Katie cautiously led the three into the misty grove. They shifted through branches, dodging boughs and limbs. They stepped around small green bushes and over the sometimes rocky, sometimes grassy ground. It was slow going; Jessie limped badly but did not complain. *I'm so sorry I got you into this,* Katie thought. She never should have told Jessie about the game. She never should have told Alex. Then maybe none of this would have happened. Katie felt anxious, anxious to keep moving, and anxious to face the dragon. Katie limped as well and her hip twinged with every step. Her right hand pulsed with pain. Poor Alex cradled his right arm across his chest to protect his sore shoulder. Would they ever forgive her for putting them through this?

They traveled quite a distance, up over hills, down into valleys and back up onto knolls, kicking up dusty puffs as they hiked along. They reached the stream and small cave where they had spent their first night. They knelt by the creek and drank the cool water with relish.

Now nearly midday, Katie found it difficult to trace the path of the sun in the sky. They sat on the cushiony sand by the stream's edge and ate the remainder of the jerky from the pack. They didn't speak; they simply sat in the warm sun and listened to the twitters and chirps of the birds. Once the sun started to move toward the west, they headed off in the opposite direction.

After hiking for a while, Katie stood at the top of a hill and saw the castle, not too far off in the distance. At the rate they traveled, they would hike through the afternoon before they would reach it. Exhaustion overshadowed her excitement to finally be near the last objective. Could they do it? Would they be able to get the last key?

They trudged on through bushes and patches of thick leaves. Soon, they approached a thickly-forested glen, and Katie paused for a moment, wondering if they neared the forest with the vines and bog. She did not know if she had the strength to swing across branches over the mire, or if she had enough speed left within her to outrun the vines. What about Jessie and Alex? Could they? Gathering bravado from somewhere deep inside herself, Katie drew her small blade and said, "Follow me."

She led the three into the dark, thick forest. A canopy of tree limbs spread above them and blocked out the sun, making the air much cooler. Katie heard some scurries and rustlings but did not see vines, only glimpses of small, furry creatures. Maybe this wasn't the forest with the gripping twines. She kept going forward cautiously, hoping they could avoid the vines and marsh. Jessie and Alex plodded along behind her.

They lumbered up a steep hill and out of the glen. Katie stopped at the crest and stood, breathing heavily. Ahead of them, the trees thinned into a meadow and on the other side of the meadow, not too far away now, stood the citadel. The setting sun bathed the castle and its rock foundation in a pinkish glow.

Finally! But now Katie had to think of a way to get back into the castle without being seen by the guards. If they crossed the grasses, out of the cover of trees, they would be seen. They'd have to wait until dark.

Then what? Katie studied the base of the mountain and spied the large cave they had flown out of days earlier with the elf's help. Katie knew the cave led to the dragon's chamber, but they would never be able to reach the opening, not without magic.

Katie scoured the mountain. There had to be another way. She saw a smaller indentation, much farther above the other. She almost missed it because it looked like a shadow in the fading sunlight. Katie frowned and squinted to get a better look. Yes, that would do. They would have to climb over some rough rocks, but then simply step along a ledge to the cavern. She felt certain they could do it; they could at least get into the castle. Once inside, they would need to find the beast and steal the key from it. *One thing at a time, Katie.*

Katie turned back to the others. "How much dust do you have left?" she asked Jessie.

Jessie opened the velvet bag and patted its base to loosen any remaining magical particles from the cloth fibers. "Just a tiny, little bit," Jessie said, shaking her head.

Katie lifted the bag and peered inside. "Not enough to float us all the way up to that cave opening, and not enough to take us over the river either. We'll have to hop across the river on rocks. We'll wait here until it's dark. I don't want to go out in the open and possibly be seen by soldiers." Katie looked back up to the high cave. "Then we'll need some sort of light. Do you think there's enough dust for that?" Katie asked.

Jessie nodded confidently, and Katie handed the bag back to her.

"Once we get back inside," Katie said as she turned and gazed again at the citadel, "we'll have to find the dragon."

"We can follow the sloping floor again, just like we did before," Alex suggested.

"Then we have to get the key," Katie said, wincing inwardly.

"How?" Jessie asked, her voice full of doubt.

Katie sighed and reluctantly explained her plan. "I'll distract the creature. Alex, do you think you could jump on its back and cut the chain from its neck?"

Alex did not nod or shake his head — he simply stared at his sister, eyes wide with fear.

"I don't want either you or Jessie to distract the dragon," Katie continued. "I'll stand in front of it. You're not hurt as bad as Jessie, so I think it will be easier for you to jump on its back and get the key. I'll give you my knife when we get inside the castle." Alex still did not respond, so Katie went on. "I'd rather not have to put you in danger at all, but we don't have much choice."

Alex looked scared, then nodded in agreement. "I'll do it," Alex said. "I'll jump on its back." He could do it, Katie knew he could. But would she be able to dodge the dragon's flames?

"I can help distract it, too," Jessie added.

"You won't be able to run with that ankle," Katie told her friend compassionately.

"Well, you've been limping, too," Jessie said, pointing to Katie's leg.

"Okay, we'll both distract it," Katie agreed, reluctantly. She did not want to hurt Jessie's feelings by refusing to let her help. Silently, she felt it was her responsibility to get all of them out, because she had brought them into this nightmare. She would still try to protect Jessie and Alex from harm, if she could.

Katie rested at the edge of the grove. Her throat felt dry and she knew the others needed some water too, but they had none. They'd have to wait until dusk, cross the meadow and then drink from the river at the base of the mountain. Katie's stomach grumbled. She wished she had her favorite dinner, fried chicken, corn on the cob and smooth mashed potatoes covered with creamy, steaming gravy. Katie closed her eyes. Thinking about food did not help. She only wished she would have enough energy and strength to continue. She felt weak and empty. Hopefully she could dredge up enough courage to do so.

She looked to where Jessie sat. Jessie held a blade of grass between her fingers and rolled it back and forth. The end of the grass twirled in a graceful whirl. Jessie stared off across the field toward the castle, her eyes vacant, as if she weren't actually seeing the citadel, but staring at something far beyond. Jessie's ankle remained puffy; Katie hoped her friend could make it.

Alex lay on his back. He gazed up into the sky with a resilient, confident look on his face. His expression reminded Katie of a look she had often seen on Ty's face.

Katie smiled wistfully. She gazed over to the golden grasses and few rolling hills that lay between them and their objective. In the waning sunlight, Katie planned a path in her mind. They could hike through the remaining forest and meadow over to the base, hop from stone to stone across the river, then go up the craggy rocks – not a tough climb after scaling a cliff wall – and follow the ledge to the cave.

16

Katie waited until the sun completely left the sky, then carefully stepped out from the cover of branches and leaves and motioned for the others to follow. Enough light remained in the sky so that they did not need Jessie's magic yet.

The tall, reedy grass rustled as they passed through. By the time they reached the river, the sun's light had completely faded. The moon's glow provided some illumination, yet did not reveal them.

They drank from the cool water; dribbles flowed down Katie's chin and she rubbed them away with the shoulder of her cloth tunic. Then Katie, Jessie and Alex began scouring the river's surface, looking for glistening stones among the water. Jessie hopped from the bank onto a stone, then, in spite of her injured ankle, gracefully leaped from one rock to another until she had reached the other side. Katie and Alex followed her path, safely bounding across the river.

Once she stood on the other side, Katie turned to the left where a huge pile of rough gray rocks led up to the ledge. Katie planted her right foot firmly, then leaned forward and reached for the top of the stone. She pushed off the ground with her left leg, ignoring the pain, and progressed up. She glanced back behind her after a few feet and made sure Jessie and Alex followed. Their heads bobbed up and down as they pressed up with their legs and stretched their arms out and up, pulling themselves along.

The day's heat radiated from the stone. The rock's surface felt warm on Katie's palms and fingertips and warmed her feet through the soles of her damp boots.

A few more lunges and Katie stood on the ledge. She shuffled onto the pebbly ground and turned back toward the others. She leaned down and extended her arm for Jessie, and Jessie grasped Katie's hand. Katie pulled her friend up. She then waited for her brother and helped him as well.

They stood on the ledge and rested for a moment. Jessie leaned back against the rock wall and breathed heavily. Katie noticed that Jessie lifted her right leg slightly off the ground to ease the pressure and pain.

"You okay?" Katie asked Jessie and Alex. She wanted to make sure the others could go on.

Jessie nodded and stuck her right thumb up into the air. Alex breathed in short, deep breaths and nodded as well. Satisfied that Jessie and Alex were as ready as they'd ever be, Katie approached the opening to the cave and peered inside. She saw nothing but darkness.

"I think we're ready for that light now," Katie said, turning back to Jessie.

Jessie unbound the velvet bag and swept her fingers around inside. She brought her hand back out; only a few sparkles glittered on her fingers and in the palm of her right hand. She cupped her left hand around her right, and then she closed her eyes and tipped her head back. She breathed deeply. Katie watched as a bluish glow slowly sent small beams through her fingers. Jessie opened her hands and a small, but very bright, light-blue orb rested in her palm. The orb rose from her hands and floated just above Jessie's right shoulder.

The three advanced into the cave, Katie in the lead, Jessie in the middle with the orb hovering over her, and Alex in the back. Would this cave be a dead end? Or would it empty out just a few feet away from the dragon's den? As they traveled quietly down the dark corridor, Katie wondered if they would be able to get the final key and exit the game.

Jessie's small orb began to dim, its light slowly fading away. Katie silently willed that it should continue to glow and provide them light just a little farther, because ahead of her she saw the end to the tunnel. The opening at the end of the passage glimmered with a yellow glow. As they approached, Katie saw the flickering of flames chase shadows across the stone walls.

Katie motioned for the others to stay back. She wanted to be sure that no soldiers patrolled the hallway. She stepped out into the lighted corridor, swiftly glancing from left to right. It was empty except for the torches stuck in brackets every few feet, providing light. Katie motioned for the others to join her, and they cautiously stepped from the darkness and entered the corridor.

The blue orb above Jessie's shoulder faded and puffed out, disappearing in a lazy wave of rising smoke. Katie silently thanked the orb for lighting their way as long as it could. She then followed the corridor to the right because the floor sloped downward slightly.

They quietly and cautiously stepped through the cold passageway. Up ahead, she heard echoing voices. She froze and stuck her left arm out to stop Jessie and Alex. Katie quickly led them to the left, and they walked swiftly yet noiselessly so as not to give themselves away. The approaching voices sounded louder but then passed by an archway and trailed off into the many halls. Katie sighed with relief, looked back at the two behind her and rolled her eyes.

She continued leading them down the sloping stone floor. At the next juncture, Katie stepped into a hallway but quickly slipped back as she saw a soldier standing guard to her left at the opposite end. Luckily the guard stood with his back toward Katie. Katie motioned for Alex and Jessie to go back the way they had come. However, wide-eyed and full of fright, they froze again as they heard voices coming from behind. Katie paused for a moment. Should they attempt to go out into the corridor where the soldier stood? Should they risk it while his back remained toward them? They had no choice; the voices behind them drew nearer. Katie quietly stepped into the corridor and, turning right, tiptoed softly down the passageway behind the soldier and out of his sight.

Katie stopped suddenly at the end of the hall before advancing into the next passage. She felt Jessie run into her back. Katie thought Jessie must have been looking behind and did not notice Katie had stopped. As Jessie bumped into Katie, a small noise escaped from her. Katie quickly looked behind her, hopeful that the soldier would not have heard the sound. The helmeted head turned slightly. The man paused for a second as if concentrating, then turned his head fully in their direction. His eyes widened and he shouted.

Katie grabbed Jessie and Alex and pulled them forward with her, but froze when she looked to her right and saw a group of soldiers at the end of a long corridor. Katie snagged Jessie and Alex's clothing at their shoulders and shoved them ahead and over to the left. She did not have to tell them to run. Alex led the way, turning quickly at each junction. The sounds of soldier's shouts, clatter of armor and tromping of heavy boots echoed in the passageways.

The three sprinted quickly down the corridor until it emptied out into a large hall. They blasted into the room, breathless. Katie instantly heard thundering footsteps in the hallways on the opposite side of the large room. They would soon be surrounded in front and behind by the advancing, relentless guards.

Katie unsheathed her knife instinctively, knew it would be useless but felt it necessary to hold the blade, and motioned for the others to stand behind her as she circled. A flood of soldiers clamored into the room and formed a ring surrounding Katie, Jessie and Alex. Katie glanced this way and that, her heart beating in her throat as the guards, with their swords drawn, closed in around them.

"No! I want them alive!" A hoarse shout erupted from behind the troops.

A few soldiers glanced over their shoulders and parted to let someone through. A tall man with gray-black hair strode through the ranks.

Fear flashed through Katie as she watched the man approach. She recognized him as the same creepy man who acted apart from the game and had scanned the throne room with his dark eyes and seemed to know they were hiding behind the drapes. Before he had left the throne room, his mouth had turned up in a strange, sly smile. He wore the same smile now.

The mysterious man stood in front of Jessie, and she tried to stare back defiantly but lowered her head, unable to meet his gaze. He seemed pleased that he disturbed her. Next, he studied Alex. Alex proudly looked back with his chin jutting out. A scoffing sound escaped the man's throat and he snorted like a beast. Then he confronted Katie and stared at her with his intense obsidian eyes. A dreadful eeriness soaked through her, and suddenly she knew it had been this character, this presence, she had felt in other parts of the game. Had it been him all along? Had it ever been Ty?

"You will not need that," the man stated and stepped up to Katie. He gripped her wrist and roughly pried the small weapon from her grip. "Bring them," the man ordered and turned quickly, exiting the room.

Two soldiers grabbed Katie's upper arms and led her away. She shuffled and pulled against the grip of the guard's hands. She twisted about and looked behind her. Two guards gripped Alex's upper arms and quickly escorted him forward. Two others grasped Jessie, and the guards swiftly marched along with her in tow.

Katie looked forward and saw the torchs' flames shiver as she and the soldiers passed by. Dread and foreboding filled her being. Where were they taking them? What would happen to them now?

She had been so worried about how they were going to get the sixth key; now she wondered if they could escape from this man. What had the king called him? Grevnon?

The guards pulled Katie, Alex and Jessie along a stone hallway, and at its end stood a large, wooden double door. The soldiers swung the doors open with a creak and a thud, and stepped inside. They kept a tight grip on Katie's arms, so tight she felt her pulse against the soldiers' fingers.

The gray-haired man had entered the room before them and swept grandly around in the center, arms extended and head back, eyes closed.

"Sir," one of the soldiers dared to speak. "The prisoners are here."

"I know, I know," Grevnon replied, irritated. He lowered his head and arms, then flipped his right hand up over his shoulder and commanded, "Leave us."

The soldiers let Katie loose, and she tried to step closer to Jessie and Alex to protect them but could not budge. She struggled to raise her arms out away from her sides, but an invisible force immobilized her. She could only shift her eyes to the side and look at Alex and Jessie, standing stiff, held in place by the same unseen force. The soldiers exited and the large doors slammed shut with a hollow thud. Torches on the walls fluttered and glowed, providing the only light in the room.

The man stalked closer to Jessie, and she tried not to tremble and quake.

Katie, desperate to protect her frightened friend, shouted, "Who are you?"

He stopped and directed his distressful gaze to Katie. Katie caught her breath and inhaled sharply. Then she tried to put on a brave, confident demeanor as the man stepped closer to her.

"I am the game," the man rumbled with pride.

Katie gasped silently. "What do you mean?" she cautiously asked, not sure she had heard him correctly.

"The others call me 'Grevnon,' but I am the game," he said in a low, rumbling voice.

Katie frowned with disbelief. Grevnon studied the three in front of him as if they were specimens in a laboratory. His gaze paused at Jessie, and he lifted his right hand and beckoned the teen toward him. Jessie glided forward, the force moving her closer to the man. Jessie cried out with fear and distress and tried to wriggle loose from the unseen grip.

"What do you want with us?" Katie shouted, intent on distracting him away from poor Jessie.

Grevnon gazed at her for a long moment and finally tipped his head slightly, as if he agreed to respond to her question.

"My 'brain,' if you will, determined a short while ago that it was being crammed with information about you beings," he said, accentuating the word "beings" with total disgust. "I became curious and one day I asked my creator what you were called. He replied 'human.' I then asked if I was 'human' and my creator replied no, that although our brains both operate with electrical impulses, I was not human. When I asked what I was, he replied 'a computer program.'" Grevnon breathed deeply, now staring directly at Katie, his dark eyes glistening as he spoke with deep intensity. "The way my creator said 'a computer program,' I sensed that I was less than 'human.'" His voice became quiet, yet each word he expelled remained as sharp as the edge of a sword. "I asked my creator, 'What must I do to become human?' He replied that it was impossible. When I pressed him for an answer, desperate to hear what I must do, my creator replied, 'You must have a soul.' When I asked what a 'soul' was, my creator did not answer. His silence angered me. How must I obtain something without knowledge of it? My creator would not explain 'soul' to me. Then began my quest to find a soul. I studied you humans until I thought I had found it. With you, Katie."

Katie straightened. He had spoken her real name! Her spine felt like it had been set on fire.

Grevnon continued. "I thought I had finally found it. You mourn for one who lost his soul and whose body became empty. Your brother, Ty."

Katie felt the blood rush from her face and her knees weakened. He knew about Ty! How could he?

"It became clear to me," Grevnon said, "that the soul exists separate from the body, but also as part of it. What is the soul except that which pushes the body to achieve? What better proof of a soul is there than the truth of it fighting *against* the body for thirst and hunger? It is the soul that pushes the body to climb up a cliff or the side of a mountain, and to strive on until it can function no longer. When the body no longer operates, or becomes damaged beyond repair, the soul escapes. The soul is so powerful, no wonder it sets you apart. I had to capture a soul and make it my own. I had to devise a plan from which I could obtain a soul, so I drew you into the game and trapped you here."

Katie stared at Grevnon, deeply frightened and disbelieving. Could a computer program trap flesh and blood humans in a virtual world? "How?" Katie breathed.

Grevnon's gaze intensified as he explained, "I have captured your electrical impulses and separated your consciousness from your physical selves. I have no doubt that I can make your souls a part of me."

A surge of fear flooded through Katie. Was that why they looked like zombies while playing? Was that why they could walk forever in the game and not move an inch in reality? How could he do this? This couldn't be happening!

Grevnon slunk nearer to Jessie and Alex. Jessie cringed as he approached.

"If you want a soul, take mine!" Katie yelled, her voice cracking.

She did not want him to threaten her friend or her brother.

Grevnon's piercing eyes turned to her and dug deep. "You have a strong soul, yes." He nodded as he stepped closer to Katie.

Katie gulped. "Let the others out of here and I will allow you to take my soul without a fight."

Alex and Jessie cried out as one, "No!" and looked at Katie with disbelief.

Grevnon shook his head. "But I don't want *your* soul," he grumbled. "Yours is imperfect." He again stepped closer to poor, trembling Jessie. "I want a soul untainted."

"What do you mean, untainted?" Katie cried, desperate to distract him and save her friend in any way she could.

"Your soul is strong. It has caring, determination, and love. But deep within you, in the shadows, are hidden feelings. Emotions and thoughts you know are there, yet you deny them. You know they pervade your thinking, your life, your soul, but you lock them away into a dark corner and try to ignore them. These emotions and thoughts taint your soul and make it imperfect." He motioned to Jessie. "She hides nothing. And neither does he." Grevnon opened his hand toward Alex, then turned back to Katie. "You know what I speak of. You keep it hidden so that not even I can see."

Katie's jaw slacked and her eyes grew wide and sad with shock, fear and deep heartache. She *did* know. After a short pause Katie whispered, "Yes."

Grevnon stepped closer to her and held out his hand, an expression of curiosity and intrigue beaming from his face as he said, "Then tell me. Tell me what else a soul can hold."

Tears welled up in Katie's eyes. Memories of purple popsicles, bike rides and laughter flooded her soul. She blinked and the tears slid down her cheeks. She licked her lips and tasted the sweet salt of her tears. "I can't," she mumbled, her chin quivering and her throat nearly closing.

"Of course you can," Grevnon said as he stepped closer and placed his hand on her shoulder in an act of false compassion.

A power, or energy — like an electric current — flowed from his touch through her shoulder and arm. Katie tried to move away and in doing so, she found that the invisible force had disappeared. But, she could not step back from him, and the weight of horrible grief removed all remaining strength. It weakened her legs and she dropped to the gray stone floor on her knees. Katie covered her face with her hands and sobbed great soul-wrenching sobs. Her body rocked forward and jerked with each wail, then rose slightly as she gasped for air.

"Tell me," Grevnon entreated, his voice quiet and sticky sweet. He raised his arm as if to pry the words from her.

Katie crumpled and cried out. She rocked on her knees and crossed her arms over her stomach, moaning terribly. She fought against his power, yet felt that it would draw out all of her hidden emotions.

"It is your brother, is it not?" Grevnon asked. "Tell me. I must feel all of it. I must know what it is like to have a soul."

Katie shook her head slowly and blinked deeply. A sharp pain radiated through her chest as if her heart had shattered into sharp, glass pieces. "You don't want to know. It hurts," she cried. "The pain is unbearable."

"Tell me about your brother," Grevnon continued, his voice smooth and deep, a current of power flowing from him.

Katie looked up into the gray-haired man's deep obsidian eyes. She could not resist. Katie blinked a slow blink, the tired, weary blink that accompanies the realization of something obvious and dreadful. She hesitated, yet she knew what he wanted. He wanted the very depths of her soul — everything — even the feelings that lurked hidden in the dusty, dark corners.

So she allowed the emotions to come forward, and their shadowy forms emerged from the darkness and showed themselves in all their horrid reality.

A thousand pleasant memories swept to the side as the shadow figures advanced. She let the feelings surface. Katie felt surprisingly calm, until the words formed on her lips and she spoke them, now overwhelmed with agony and pain, "I…hated…him."

It was done. She had said it. Katie wept heavily. The cork had been expelled from the bottle and now all the thoughts and feelings flooded out, running, screaming from the corners of her soul. Everything she had hidden inside since the day her brother had died came bursting forth. It was as if a dam of forbidden thoughts had been cracked and now crumbled away, and the torrent of emotions came flooding out as she vomited her wicked feelings.

"Ty could do nothing wrong," she said as she shook her head and sobbed. "My parents would be all smiles when they looked at his report card. Then when they'd see mine, it would be whispers and frowns. I was so… *jealous* of him."

She gripped her sides, the ache in her stomach growing. "He played trumpet perfectly," she said, grimacing. "He was really talented. I wish I could play clarinet as well. All I can do is squeak the stupid thing."

Katie spoke to the stone floor, her voice thick with disgust for her own feelings. A droplet of spittle dribbled from the corner of her mouth. She wiped her mouth with the back of her hand and continued. "Ty ran like the wind. He brought home trophies for track. I trip over my own feet." She sobbed as she released more and more of her anger and trembled. "He was everything my parents dreamed of, everything I'll never be, and now he's gone. I can't help but think that they'd rather…."

Katie cried out and curled over, resting her forehead on the cold, stone floor. She didn't care anymore. She didn't care that Jessie and Alex now knew, how she really felt. She only wanted to set Jessie and

Alex free. She sucked in a breath and straightened up, looked into Grevnon's dark eyes and swallowed hard. She spoke with a coarse, harsh voice, "You can have my soul. I don't want it anymore. You can have it with all of its imperfections. You can have all of it!"

Jessie gasped and wailed, "Katie no!" She tried to move and struggled, but could not break free of the invisible grip.

"Promise me you'll let them go!" Katie pleaded with Grevnon.

"Don't do it!" Alex shouted, his voice squeaking with emotion, as he too tried to fight the unseen force.

"All right," Grevnon spoke, his voice deep and smooth. He stepped up to Katie and placed his hands on either side of her head.

A wave of stabbing pain swept through Katie. She closed her eyes and more tears slid down her cheeks. Grevnon squeezed her head tighter, and Katie shuddered with the flood of pain, now growing in intensity and sharpness. All through her body, every inch of her cried out, and then she began to feel weight pressing throughout her chest, arms and legs, as if something tried to crush her. Grevnon gritted his teeth and grimaced with concentration as he shook Katie with intensity. Katie closed her eyes; the sight of him made her stomach churn. She fought against the pressing weight, but knew she must give in, must give in. In order to free Alex and Jessie, she must give in.

17

Grevnon crumpled to the floor in a heap. Katie blinked and frowned, but then she felt her legs beneath her stand up. She felt removed, as if she were three feet back within her skin.

"Come now," she heard herself say as her arm motioned to Jessie and Alex. "I'll show you the way out," she said sweetly.

Jessie stepped away from Katie; the invisible grip no longer held her, and she seemed confused. Alex stood back and frowned too.

"Come on," Katie said gently, motioning with her arm. She walked toward the double doors and the others followed, hesitantly.

Katie felt faint and dizzy. She didn't feel like she actually walked down the castle hall, yet she did. She felt her arms and legs move without willing them to do so. Alex walked with her on the left and Jessie on the right. Katie caught them exchanging worried glances. But they did not need to worry.

Alex grabbed his sister's arm and spoke emphatically. "You have to come with us!"

"It's all right," Katie assured her brother calmly. "Whenever you play the game, I'll be right here." She felt her cheeks press up into a forced smile. She spoke, and the words flowed without her causing them to do so. Katie led the others down the sloping floor.

"Where are we going?" Alex asked, pointing in a different direction.

"To the exit," Katie stated plainly and gripped her brother's collar.

"But I've played this level before," Alex said, trying to pull back from his sister. "The exit is that way," he said as he pointed insistently.

Katie felt her left hand grip Alex's collar tightly and force him along with her. Ahead of them, a dark cave opening loomed.

"Katie, what's happening?" Jessie demanded.

"Jessie, run away!" Alex shouted as he twisted, plucked at Katie's firm fingers and struggled against the grip on his collar. Katie felt his fingernails dig into her hand, but she did not feel pain and did not loosen her grip.

Jessie turned and ran back down the hallway in the direction of the exit, her footsteps echoing away from them as she ran.

Katie raised her head without wanting to do so and laughed a wicked laugh. "She'll never find the exit before my guards capture her." Then Katie forced Alex forward once again.

At the entrance to the cave, she snatched a torch out of its bracket on the wall and dragged the young teen into the cavern. The sounds of his shuffling and struggling echoed off the rocks.

Katie unwillingly opened her mouth and from it came an unnatural, booming voice that yelled, "Dragon!"

Alex grasped her arm and dug his fingernails in farther, attempting to pull her solid grip loose. The collar tore and Alex almost slipped away, but Katie grasped his hair and held him by the top of his head. He kicked at her legs and punched her; Katie felt the impact but no pain. She felt her brother tug and pull against her grip.

"Dragon! I have a gift for you!" Katie's unreal voice called.

Under her feet she felt the unmistakable vibrations of the creature's heavy plodding. Alex dug his nails deeper into Katie's arm and she felt warm blood seep from the wounds.

A growl sounded from the darkness ahead and Alex froze. Katie felt her brother shudder with fear. Through her eyes she watched the shadows for any motion and saw a dim, spiny head emerge from the blackness into the torchlight. Katie felt Alex inhale sharply. The dragon's black, forked tongue flashed out if its mouth toward the two. Then it slithered from the tunnel into the larger cavern. It crouched slightly and withdrew from the flame of the torch Katie held. The torchlight sparkled on its green-black scales.

Katie felt her left arm thrust her brother forward and heard herself proclaim, "I brought you a gift, great one!"

The creature's forked tongue flashed out of its huge mouth and then back again as if tasting the air around the struggling youth.

"Take him, and we shall rule this world together!" Katie shrieked and then exploded in an evil, vicious laugh.

Within herself, Katie desperately fought against the thing that had inhabited her. She could not let harm come to Alex! Katie gathered strength from within, from places Grevnon had not trod once he had possessed her, where there were even more hidden shadows of unimaginable power. Katie concentrated, feeling the power and energy within her rise against the evil. She must make him release Alex! She tried to pry her fingers loose. They felt numb and stiff, but she forced them with all her might. She concentrated, determined to let her brother go, and willed her fingers to move. Through her eyes, she studied her own hand and watched in absolute amazement as her will pried open her grip, and her brother's brown hair slipped through her fingers.

Alex scurried away from Katie. Katie wanted to yell at Alex to run, find Jessie and then find the exit, but no words would come from her mouth. Before she could regain control of herself, Katie felt hot flame shoot from the dragon and flash above her, and then the dragon reached a gigantic claw out and grasped her around the waist.

The monster lifted Katie from the floor and pulled her closer to its saliva-dripping jaws. As the dragon drew her nearer, she saw the golden key draped around its scaly neck. The sixth key, the key that could possibly free them from this awful game, was now here within her reach, yet she could not snag it from the dragon's neck. As the creature lifted her toward its dripping jaws, a shriek erupted from her. The dragon recoiled from the sound. Katie winced as well from the shrill cry and from the horrid pain in her head. It felt as if her skull would split open. She weakened as the dragon squeezed her tighter, pressing the air from her lungs, nearly crushing her ribs with its grip. As the dragon moved Katie closer to its slowly opening mouth and huge fangs, the pain increased and Katie screamed, but this time *she* willed it, and felt the screech tear at her own throat. With her shriek, a sharp pain radiated throughout her body and became excruciating, and Katie felt as if her life was slipping away. She held on with all her might and pressed the evil presence from her. She felt it flow from her, tearing at her as it went, and she cried out as it ripped away. She watched it seep from her skin, float through the air and form a sparking pool of glistening oil on the cave wall. Then it oozed onto the crags of the cave, shimmering in the flickering torchlight, and crept along the rocks until it disappeared into the shadows.

The dragon recoiled from the dark flow that had poured from Katie, but now it examined her, turning her from side to side in its claw. Katie blinked slowly and, with renewed determination, reached up and snagged the golden chain, yanking it loose from the dragon's neck. The links snapped free and Katie held the dangling chain and key in her right hand. She pushed her strong legs against the palm of the dragon's claw, trying to pry herself free, but its grip would not loosen. Slowly it raised her toward its opened, sharp-toothed jaws.

Suddenly, a fireball sliced the darkness and impacted on the dragon's head, sending sparks of red and yellow flame across the cave. The dragon howled, reared its spiny, sizzling head and shot a tongue of flame toward the dark cave ceiling. It released its grip on Katie and she dropped to the ground, thudding against the hard floor. She quickly scrambled out of the dragon's reach.

Katie watched as another yellow fireball illuminated the cave and the cringing dragon. The flaming orb impacted on the creature's back, making its scales sizzle and smoke. The dragon rose on its hind legs and shot another yellow flame toward the roof. A third bright fireball flashed against the dragon's chest. The beast yowled horribly and dropped to the ground. It moaned and groaned, then turned and retreated into the darkness of the cave.

Katie breathed a sigh of relief as the dragon lumbered away. She stood and quickly searched for Alex, using the faint light from the dropped torch.

"Alex!" she called, her voice echoing through the rugged cave. Alex stepped cautiously out from behind some rocks where he had hidden, but he kept his distance.

"It's okay," Katie assured her brother and motioned for him to step closer. "It's me — really it is me. He's gone."

"I saw it," Alex shakily admitted. "Whatever it was, I saw it leave you."

"Katie?" Jessie's voice echoed down from a perch high in the rocky cave.

"Jessie!" a very relieved Katie shouted up toward her friend. "Was that you? Did you shoot those fireballs?"

"Yeah," Jessie called down. "I found a healing elixir and drank it and got my fireballs back!"

Katie glanced down at the key swinging in her grasp. Had the game provided elixir because she'd grabbed the key? Or had the game returned to semi-normal when Grevnon had oozed away along the walls? Katie removed the five other keys from her neck and held them all together. As she studied the twinkling gold in the palm of her hand, she saw faded letters turn bright, then brighter still and even brighter until the words "Health 8%," "Weapons 0%," and "Food 0%" were displayed in front of her.

"Do you see it?" Katie asked, pointing excitedly to the air down in front of her.

"Yeah!" Alex stared, wide-eyed, down to his left and right.

Katie called up to the promontory on which Jessie stood, "How did you get up there?"

"There's a tunnel," Jessie said, and then she disappeared from the dark, rock ledge. Katie placed her arm gently across Alex's shoulders and gave him a quick hug. Then she released him and they walked back out of the cavern and into the torch-lit corridor.

They met Jessie coming toward them in the passageway. She smiled and Katie wrapped her arms around Jessie and hugged her. They had escaped Grevnon and the dragon, but they were not safe yet.

Katie then released her friend, looked over at Alex and asked, "Which way is the exit?"

Alex led the three through the musty castle halls, but then he slowed and acted cautious as they approached a large wooden door with six keyholes across the middle.

"This wasn't here before," Alex said, confused.

"Maybe it is here now because we have all the keys. How did you exit before?" Katie wondered.

"Well, if you got the key to the first level, you had to find the door with one lock, or you could choose the option to exit," Alex said, looking down toward the floor, searching for the word.

Katie did the same but shook her head; the word "exit" did not appear with the other displays of health, weapons and food. "This has got to be it," Katie breathed.

Katie quickly searched through the six keys in her hand. None had a number imprinted on it, and she did not know which one had been obtained in which of the six worlds. She held one key between finger and thumb and inserted it into the first keyhole. It turned neither to the left, nor to the right. She tried the next and the next until she found one that did turn to the right with a click. *Great, now we're getting somewhere!* She excitedly tried all five other keys, her breath quickening and her throat running dry, until she had placed each in its appropriate lock. She turned the final key to the right with a click and the door dissolved into bright light and illumination shone around the three.

Katie felt queasy and dizzy, but did not yet allow herself to feel relieved. Then the light faded, darkness swept in around them, and three large yellow words glowed in the blackness; they said "Six Levels Achieved."

A sick headache pounded in Katie's head and she felt the game pull reluctantly away from her as it released her. She reached her hand up toward her face, felt the mask and gingerly lifted it from her face. Immediately she looked to her right.

Alex swiped the mask up over his brown hair and yanked the gloves from his fingers. Jessie did the same and dropped the things to the floor of Katie's room.

Katie removed her gloves as well; she couldn't get them off her fingers quickly enough. "We made it," Katie said quietly. Then she suddenly remembered that they had spent the last few days inside a virtual reality game. She limped to her nightstand, stiff and sore, and lifted her alarm clock. It showed five-thirty. What? Had they only been away from the real world for a few hours when it had seemed like days? Was that why no one had tried to disconnect them?

"Huh, only about 2 hours have passed," Katie said, mystified.

Jessie hobbled up next to her friend and stared at the clock. "How can that be?"

"I don't know," Katie said, shaking her head.

"When we played before, time seemed to go on normally," Alex said, confused.

"I know," Katie agreed. "Wait a minute. What day is it?"

Alex looked at his watch and said quietly, "Wow. It's still today."

When Grevnon had trapped them in the game, had he caused time to practically stand still? Katie didn't know and didn't understand. It seemed so unreal. Had it all really happened? Her aching hip and hand said that it had.

"Jessie, does your ankle still hurt?" Katie asked, wondering if her friend still felt her injuries as well

Jessie nodded. "Not as bad as it did in the game, but yeah."

"Same with my shoulder," Alex said, and he massaged his right shoulder and rolled his arm.

"I don't believe it," Katie sighed and sat on her bed. It *had* really happened. Their injuries proved it, but she felt so disappointed. They had played the game in the first place because they thought they'd heard Ty. Had Ty spoken to them at all? Or had Grevnon played a trick on them to get them to go through the game?

"Do you think it ever was Ty who spoke to us? Or was it Grevnon all along?" Katie asked. "Oh, I can't believe I said those things about Ty!" Katie covered her mouth with her hand and felt her cheeks flush.

Jessie sat next to Katie and said calmly, "There are so many things you are good at. Maybe you can't play clarinet, but you are a good singer. Remember when we took choir together? You even got to do a solo. And maybe you're not good at math or other subjects, but you forget that you do pretty good in language arts. And maybe you can't run and be on the track team, but you were great at gymnastics. You quit. I didn't understand why, but now I think I do. I think you were trying to compete with him and not just be yourself."

Jessie was right, and Katie knew it. What had made her stop pursuing the things she enjoyed? Was it really a desire to compete with Ty? Why couldn't she have just been happy doing the things she liked? Was it pride? Stubbornness? Suddenly, she knew she had really never hated Ty. She had hated not being able to bring home trophies and awards. Maybe she could have won a trophy for gymnastics. She quit before she had given herself a chance.

"Don't ever think that we'd rather you were gone, Katie," Alex added, shaking his head slowly. "I want you here." Alex sighed heavily. "I want Ty back, too."

"Me too," Katie agreed and felt tears form in her eyes.

They sat in Katie's room in silence for a few minutes and then Jessie finally said, "I'd better get home. I'm sorry, Katie. I'm sorry it wasn't him."

"I'm sorry, too. And I'm sorry you got hurt. I never meant for you to get hurt," Katie said, motioning to Jessie's ankle. "And it was crazy anyway to hope to find Ty in the game."

"No, I don't think it was," Jessie said, smiling. "And I think the pain will go away. I'm already feeling a little better."

Katie walked her friend down the stairs to the front door. Katie asked Jessie to call when she got home, then Katie hobbled up the stairs and toward her doorway. She heard Alex rummaging around in his room. Back to their normal routine? But she knew they would never be the same.

Katie entered her room and stared at the TV screen. She still could not believe what had happened to them. If Alex and Jessie had not been there with her, she would have thought that she had lost it. But it *did* happen, and all those terrible things…well, she had said them. She hadn't imagined any of it.

She felt strangely and yet comfortably free. Was it because she had released all the horrid jealousies and hate she had felt toward her brother? Yes. She had let it go, and now unspeakable relief flowed from her heart to every corner of her soul. But she also felt pain and anguish. Ty was gone.

The phone rang and Katie answered it quickly, hoping it was Jessie.

"Hello?" Katie asked.

"It's me," Jessie replied.

"You got home okay. Good. Oh, Jessie, I feel so stupid now. Can you ever forgive me? Do you think he could ever forgive me for saying those things? I'm such an idiot. I can't believe it," Katie rambled.

"Don't worry about it," Jessie calmly replied. "You have just lost your brother. You have a lot of feelings rushing through you. I don't think any differently about you. Maybe now I know why you did certain things, like quit choir and gymnastics, but don't worry about it."

How could she always be right? "Thanks, Jessie," Katie whispered. "You'll never know how much that means to me."

"Go to sleep now. I'll call you in the morning," Jessie said.

"Talk to you later," Katie replied quietly.

Go to sleep. She couldn't go to sleep. She wanted to tell Mom and Dad – what would she tell them? That she, Jessie and Alex had been trapped in a virtual world, and that the virtual reality game had tried to possess her soul and made her reveal insane jealousies concerning her deceased brother? Crazy!

What did she want to tell them? Nothing about the game. Nothing about jealousy. What she really wanted to do was just talk. They hadn't talked since Ty had died. They had all dealt with their anguish and pain without words and Katie suddenly felt that was wrong. She knew that recognizing her hidden feelings had helped her. She wanted to talk – and to listen. Maybe it would help Mom and Dad?

She walked quietly down the stairs and into the living room. Dad sat in the recliner, his mouth open and his eyes closed. He had fallen asleep. Katie quietly slipped into the kitchen.

"Hi, Katie," her mother greeted her, looking up briefly from her cup of tea.

Katie slid into the chair next to her mother. "Mom?" Katie hesitantly asked.

"Yes?" Audry replied, staring into her cup.

Katie didn't speak, so her mother slowly raised her head and looked into Katie's eyes with a gentle frown. "Can we talk about Ty?" Katie asked.

Audry reached over and embraced Katie, hugging her tight. When she pulled back, Audry's eyes brimmed with tears and she nodded as if she too, had been waiting for the right moment to release all of her fears and worries, all of her dragons of the soul.